A KILLING IN RETROSPECT

A SISTER MARY AGNES MYSTERY

A KILLING IN
RETROSPECT

BARBARA CUMMINGS

FIVE STAR
A part of Gale, Cengage Learning

GALE
CENGAGE Learning™

Detroit • New York • San Francisco • New Haven, Conn • Waterville, Maine • London

GALE
CENGAGE Learning™

LIBRARY OF CONGRESS CATALOGING-IN-PUBLICATION DATA

Cummings, Barbara.
  A killing in retrospect : a Sister Mary Agnes mystery / Barbara Cummings. — 1st ed.
    p. cm.
  ISBN-13: 978-1-59414-784-5 (alk. paper)
  ISBN-10: 1-59414-784-1 (alk. paper)
    1. Nuns—Fiction. 2. Catholics—Fiction. 3. Rhode Island—Fiction. I. Title.
PS3603.U655K54 2009
813'.6—dc22   2009019363

First Edition. First Printing: October 2009.
Published in 2009 in conjunction with Tekno Books and Ed Gorman.

To the nuns of St. Frances Xavier Academy, who taught generations of Rhode Island girls that they had value and worth in their role as daughters of God. The school is no longer there; but you will forever be loved, admired, and respected by those whose lives you touched.

To four women who give selflessly to make this world a better place and who truly enrich my life—my sister Janet McElroy; my sisters-in-law, Ann Malmborg and Toby Galli; and, last but never least, my best friend, Nancy Martin. I love you all.

To my Dad, my childhood refuge. You were all I had when Mommy died, and all I needed.

And to Rhode Island. Home.

CHAPTER ONE

According to anyone you asked in Rhode Island, in this, Hoover's Depression, we Merciful Sisters of Mary led fairly easy, ordinary lives. We prayed. We taught the parish children at St. Catherine's Academy. We ate regular, healthy meals. We worked hard. We laughed often. Life was good.

Most of the time.

But there were other times when—quite literally and quite unexpectedly—a little bit of hell bubbled up. Slowly. Imperceptibly. A sneaky little demon on the hunt.

We were almost through with the last of our lessons for the day when Mother Frances's new assistant, and a new novice to boot, streamed pell-mell into my classroom, out of breath and google-eyed. And not a good google, like the funny men, Ben Turpin and Eddie Cantor; more like one of the gargoyles in the church, the one that gave me the willies. When Sister Rosalia braced her slightly pudgy self on the door frame, patting her bosom and fanning her face, she had the attention of my entire fourth-grade class, and most of them were almost as google-eyed as she.

I hurried up the aisle and shushed a couple of the students, one of whom—Eugenio Carcieri—was imitating the gargoyle, with crossed eyes, stretched lips and stuck-out tongue.

Saints preserve us and Lord give me strength! What were we to do with this silly novice? There was only room for one resident whirlwind in our convent, and according to Mother Frances, one, *me*, was more than enough.

Within a blink, my companion and best friend, Sister Winifred, poked her head through the connecting double doors between our classrooms. She certainly had what our students called her bat ears tuned high that afternoon. With those ears, she could hear the rustle of long black skirts and the *click-click-click* of a wooden rosary from a block away. No doubt she could also count the rapid beats of Sister Rosalia's heart.

She took one look at Rosalia's wind-reddened cheeks and turned to me, raising her eyebrows in her inimitable way that I could read very well.

"I didn't do anything," I asserted, but I kept my fingers crossed for luck.

Winifred snorted and elevated her elegant left eyebrow to the edge of her starched and neatly pressed wimple. "Let's just let the young sister confirm that, shall we?"

Under our combined well-rehearsed, steely-eyed stares, Rosalia caught her breath quickly. "It's Reverend Mother. She got a call on that new telephone, shut her office door with a bang, and has been muttering aloud to herself the last ten minutes. She told me to come get you and for Sister Winifred to keep an eye on your class."

This time, Winnie whistled softly before she laughed. "Didn't do anything, indeed. You'll probably get more than just kitchen duty for this—whatever it is. Let's just hope there isn't another incident like that poor girl in the cold cellar."

"I'll be right back," I told Winnie.

"Sure you will." She patted my slumped shoulders, knowing full well I was Daniel going into the lion's den. "Don't worry. The children will be fine."

But will I?

Winnie checked to make sure her students were quiet as church mice, then sang out happily to my fourth-graders, "Let's have a quick vocabulary quiz, class."

As I walked from the classroom, I raised my eyes to the ceiling and beyond. *Care to give me a hint what this is about, Lord? No? Any time soon? Why not!?* Darn my socks, other than my almost unnoticeable twitching at breakfast, I could swear I did everything I was supposed to do, and nothing I wasn't.

Sister Rosalia hitched up her voluminous skirts and bolted ahead. The minx. Younger and stronger. She'd soon learn my Irish grandmothers' rules of thumb: When others are running, walk. When others are walking, stand. When others are standing, sit. When others are sitting, lie down. Yep, Irish grandmothers went into life with individuality and gusto, as long as it didn't involve actual expenditure of energy.

This afternoon, hurrying after Rosalia, I was expending enough energy for every Irish grandmother in Rhode Island. But would I have enough energy left over to deal with Mother Frances and whatever latest dire deed she thought I'd committed?

The short walk down the stairs and out onto the stony walkway that separated the school from the convent grounds usually calmed me. Not today. This was the way the last contretemps had started. Oh, not from a summons but, instead, from another of Mother Frances' orders. That time ended with my finding a poor dead girl atop the carrots in the cold cellar, and it didn't end until all those responsible were found and arrested. Six dead. Five arrested. The scales didn't balance if I considered only that. But there were also the children who had been rescued from tyranny, three of whom were being adopted by my cousin Josiah. Once again I raised my head, but this time with a grateful *Thank You* instead of a question. *Now if you could just run interference with Mother Frances, tonight I'll start making a dent in some of those rosaries I owe you. On my knees. Honest.*

What *had* I done wrong?

"Are you in trouble, Sister Agnes?"

I turned at the question to find my favorite student, Dante Ricci, staring up at me with a tearful sheen sparking his sensitive, big brown eyes. I reached out my hand and he took it, giving it a comforting squeeze. "Don't worry," I told him. "It's nothing bad."

"You sure?"

No, but I'm trying to be. I shrugged. That shrug was a child's usual answer, but it would do for now. "And what are you doing here, little man? Aren't you supposed to be taking a vocabulary test?"

He shook his head. "It was only a quiz and I knew all the words, so Sister said I could go find Richard since there's only a few more minutes until the dismissal bell."

Richard was Richard DelVecchio, who was assigned by Dante's father to drive him to and from school, and just about anywhere else the young motherless boy wanted to go. Dante's father? Vincent Gaetano Ricci. Reputed mob boss. Although . . . Vincent had never been caught doing anything illegal. Not once. Some of his "associates," yes; but never him. All of it was either vicious rumor or he was the most well-protected businessman in little old Rhody. Whatever the truth, from personal experience I knew him to be a loyal friend to Richard and a loving, attentive father. If he did dastardly things, I didn't know for certain. *Judge not, right, Lord? Yes, I'll keep my head screwed on tight, just in case. Thanks for the advice.*

Dante bolted ahead as soon as he caught sight of Richard's tall, lanky form lounging against the side of Vincent's big ivory and maroon-trimmed Lincoln town car. Richard waved and scooped Dante into his arms. "Good luck, Aggie! You're gonna need it!"

Grrrr. He always seemed to know more than I did about the comings and goings at the convent. I was beginning to think he had a spy in the midst of all us penguins, as he called us.

The head penguin saw me coming. Tapping her foot in agitation was only one sign that I'd best act the self-effacing nun she had been trying her darnedest to turn me into. So far, it was but a wish and a prayer.

Mother Frances was a head taller than I and slightly pudgier. Her clear blue eyes and flawless porcelain complexion outshined my peachy cheeks and grey-blue eyes, the kind that look muddy. That complexion and sky-blue eyes were what drew attention to her first. It was, actually, the only thing that any of us had that was more than serge, starched cotton, and clunky black brogans. However, I was most envious of her thin and elegant foot, but not when—like now—it was *tap, tap, tap*ping her impatience.

"Second time today, Sister Agnes."

I cringed inside, but dared not show my trepidation. She was referring to my lack of attention at this morning's scripture reading, of course. I couldn't help it. It was one of St. Paul's letters, and the man could truly rant on. I got a mite twitchy, thought I hid it well, but obviously Mother Frances had been vigilant and less than pleased. Why else was I here? I was waiting for her axe to drop, wondering what my punishment was going to be. But that hardly accounted for her pulling me out of class in such a hurry. She could whack my head off any time. So what was up?

"Sit," she ordered, pointing to the least comfortable chair in her office. I sat gingerly on the edge of the seat so I wouldn't get any splinters in my nether regions and leaned forward as she sank into her own hard swivel chair. She pursed her lips and glanced from me to the portrait of Saint Catherine, which adorned the wall opposite her desk. It was the only vivid thing in this large but monotone office. Boring beige must have been a great bargain. The walls blended into beige upholstery on burnished oak furniture. The room had an erased look about it, as if it were holding forth an example for us to follow. Erased. All personality eliminated. Hence, the sameness of our head-to-foot covering. But sadly, that hadn't erased my exuberance or cockeyed view of the world outside these convent walls—and in.

Sighing, Mother Frances closed her eyes and shivered, which gave me goose bumps. She never showed emotion, except anger, so before she spoke I knew there was trouble.

"We've got problems," she said.

"We?"

Her eyes popped open. I was really in trouble. Mother Frances' startling robin's egg blue hue had darkened almost to navy. "Sister!"

"Sorry, Reverend Mother. You were saying . . . ?"

"The Chancery called with a request."

"One you can't refuse?"

"Indeed; but more one *you* can't refuse." She slid open the center drawer on her desk and handed me a large envelope. "This came last week."

I recognized the navy blue edging on the left side and the interesting individualized crest atop it, sort of a coat of arms; but who had a real coat of arms with a chicken and a brimmed cap on it? What I held in my hands was the invitation to Dante Ricci's late mother, Catherine Ricci's, Anniversary Mass two weeks from this coming Saturday. One year ago she had died in what was officially deemed an accident, although not many people believed the accidental part. Some even went so far as to suggest that she had been in the wrong place at the wrong time and it was actually her husband who was meant to die.

"I've seen that," I said. "Richard showed it to me a few weeks ago. The Ricci family is inviting scores of people."

"Yes. Family, politicians, business associates, and friends. They're expecting so many to attend . . ." She didn't need to say that some of those attendees would be unscrupulous. Her tone said it all. ". . . that they almost booked the cathedral. But as you can see from the invitation, they've decided that they want her Mass to be here, at St. Catherine's."

"Well, that's appropriate. St. Catherine is Catherine Ricci's namesake and patron saint, and this was her home parish."

"Yes. Which is why the parish is being so honored." Once more, that sigh and shiver. "We—all of us nuns—have been asked to attend also. En masse."

"That's nice."

"It might be, if they hadn't also requested a command performance by you."

"Performance? At a Memorial Mass?" I caught my breath at the possibility of what she was saying. "Surely they wouldn't allow a woman to assist at Mass."

"Don't be silly. That will never happen." She steepled her hands together and sighed. "What they want is . . ." This time she actually shuddered. She was going to need a warming pan in her bed tonight. "Oh, there's no other easy way to say this. They want all of us to serve as the choir, and they want *you* to sing the responses."

My heart took a vacation; and my stomach quickly followed. I stared at her, my mouth slightly agape. But try as I might, I couldn't shut it. No wonder Richard had been so chipper. He knew what was coming all right. And he knew the fiasco that would ensue if . . . *If?* . . . What was I thinking? "I can't do it."

"Everyone here at St. Catherine's knows that. But those at the Chancery do not. I tried to come up with a good excuse, but there was no way I could refuse this entreaty. Monsignor Grace will officiate and he called personally to have me importune you."

Wow! That must have left a bad taste in her mouth—like the pork roast I'd tried to fix on my cooking rotation. All pepper, no taste. I was the worst nun in the whole danged convent.

Couldn't cook. Couldn't iron. Couldn't concentrate on the morning readings. Couldn't stay awake in chapel. Had more pins in my torn clothing than thread and spit. Talked to God, sometimes aloud, as if He were in the room, and owed him more prayers than I could ever send to him in a lifetime. Right now, worst of all these failings, I had never been able to find middle C; not even if my life depended on it. Which, apparently, it did.

"I can't sing!"

As if her mere words could magically make it happen, she ordered, "You *will* sing. You will practice every morning and every night and during any free time you have for the next two weeks."

"Mother Frances, surely you remember the sounds I make, even when I try my darnedest not to." Her mouth pursed up as if she were sucking on a lemon. She remembered. I reached out my hand and discovered it was shaking like a birch branch during a nor'easter. *Oh, Lord, why me?* "Please. Can't we all do this together?"

I truly tried to convince her to excuse me and when that did no good, pleaded with God to stop time. Unfortunately, He thought the rules of the universe were too important to change for a panic-stricken nun. So, two weeks later, a little off to the edge of the altar seats nearest the nave where the congregation sat waiting for the Mass to begin, I stood dead center, listening for the notes that would precede my "performance."

Could anyone die of pure stage fright—especially a nun? Yes!

No! No, no, no, no, no! There will be no dying today. I, Sister Mary Agnes, simply had to ignore that dull ache behind my breastbone. Those racing beats? Didn't mean a thing. And that hard and loud booming? Not important. No one could hear them; so they wouldn't spoil the introductory notes of Catherine Ricci's Memorial Mass. I raised my eyes to heaven. *From my thoughts to your ears, Father. Please.*

Darn my socks! My personal phone line to the Lord must have been a party line that morning. Mother Frances glared at me as if she had heard every word of my distressed missive to the Lord. Okay, so I was nervous. After all, I'd had two weeks to get to full crash-and-burn mode. Winnie, in her inimitable way, had ordered me to suck it in.

"Just take one deep breath and let it out," she'd said this morning as she adjusted my veil, which, as usual, was listing, exposing my white caplet. Twelve years in the convent and I still needed help dressing. There was simply no hope for me. I should have been able to accept that, but I came from stolid stock that didn't give in easily. It could lead to feuds or fanfare. I was betting on feuds.

One deep breath. Right. As if it were that easy. There were hundreds of people in the church, and they would all be listening to me.

Me!

Oh, for crying out loud, this was silly. I'd been a nun for almost half my life. And although she didn't have to, after my concerted pleading and a trickle of forced tears, Mother Frances had appealed to the Chancery. When she explained my complete lack of talent and the many faux pas I had committed in the name of music, Monsignor Grace had laughed long and loud—truly. I heard him on the party line when I listened in on Mother's phone call, *and, yes, I will do penance for that, Lord*—but he had agreed that I only had to sing one word. One word? Hah! It was five sustained, ascending syllables, but technically it *was* only one word.

Only one word.

Only. One. Word.

I could do this.

I hoped.

The bells rang the monsignor's entry from the sacristy. Everyone rose as he positioned himself facing the massive crucifix above the altar and raised his right hand to his forehead for the introductory sign of the cross. His tenor rang as loud and as clear as the last peal of the bell in St. Catherine's bell tower. *"In nomine Patris . . ."* He touched his breastbone—where there were probably no loud booms jostling *his* chest. *". . . et Filii . . ."* Now his left shoulder. *". . . et Spiritus . . ."* Then his right shoulder. *". . . Sancti . . ."*

As if we had rehearsed it a million times—which, of course, we had—eleven Merciful Sisters of Mary quietly accompanied my much louder five note *Amen* response. I opened my mouth and pushed the first *ah* out. *Hey, not bad!* I had missed several meals and back-to-back hectic days away from the usual convent chores, just to rehearse this one small task. A million times. I'd sung this Amen a million times, and it sounded as if it was going to be okay. I looked into the eyes of God, as evidenced in the fresco above the crucifix. *Thanks.* The Good Lord was still right in there pitching—no pun intended—when my second *ah* ascended two octaves. A little wobbly, but acceptable. At the third ascension, however, the *ah* sounded like a strangled chicken. The fourth *ah* cracked completely. Though I tried, to save my soul I couldn't get the final *men* in human auditory range. Probably every dog for miles was howling. Luckily the sisterhood choir elevated their voices as I lost mine. As usual, my heart was in it, but my vocal chords were weak.

Lord, I am heartily sorry for having offended thee.

And Vincent Ricci and the entire New England underworld.

Not sorry enough, I guess. At that last strangled chicken sound, Richard DelVecchio craned his neck to catch my eye. His eyebrows scored a touchdown with his mop of blond hair. His mustache twitched. Oooooh, at that very moment I really hated mustaches. Then, as if I wasn't embarrassed enough, in front of everyone, his big body shook with laughter.

Darn his socks!

And all his unmentionables, too!

In a blink, Dante's face collapsed and he slumped down in his seat. Usually, Richard kept a close watch over his charge. But this time Richard was laughing too hard—at me. He didn't see the boy slip over the edge of his seat and scoot under it. But Mother Frances, who the students at St. Catherine's Academy said had coyote eyes, didn't miss a thing. She turned her head to find me and nodded towards Dante, who by now had shimmied on his belly to the next aisle and was crawling towards the side altar. His father seemed oblivious to the departing boy. Who could fault him? After all, this Mass was dedicated to his beloved late wife.

As the reporters and photographers positioned outside could attest, hundreds had come from all over New England to pay respects, or out of a sense of duty or fear. Like good Italian Catholics, they were paying attention to the ritual of the Mass, if not its meaning. They were too engrossed to notice the small figure pick up speed and dart behind a stone pillar leading to the side altar. Mother Frances snapped her sleeves at me in her inimitable "step-to-it" demand. I suppose she could have gone after Dante herself, but the lonely boy and I had become close during that awful time a few months ago when there was murder and mayhem on the convent grounds. She was right to send me. So I carefully edged behind Sister Winifred into the gloom of the sacristy waiting area, where the priests and altar boys prepared themselves for Mass. It was close to the hall leading to the side altar dedicated to St. Catherine, and I could hear a scuttling sound that I associated with *boy*.

"Dante?"

I heard a little moan followed by a sniff and found him in front of the rack of candles, trying to reach high above his head for a taper to light a candle to St. Catherine. "Here, let me do that." He held my hand while I dipped the slim taper into a large cobalt glass holding a lit candle. The wick flared, and I then carefully transferred the flame to another candle before I blew out the taper.

"Nonno says you need to put money in the box."

Nonno was his grandfather, old and wizened and wise, who was intermittently confined to a private hospital because of terrible lung problems. "Do you have money of your own?"

"Yes, but Richard has it."

"Well . . ." I dug into my pocket and came up with two crumpled handkerchiefs and three nickels. I handed one to Dante.

"Richard puts in a quarter," he said as he dropped the coin into the slot. It clanked against the side before settling to the bottom.

"Richard has money to burn."

Dante smiled slightly, then bowed his head in prayer as the flame flickered and bounced until it burned up to a nice cleansing fire. At the conclusion of his short prayer, his hand tightened on mine as he looked up at me. "I wanted to ask you something."

"Yes?"

"It's important."

"Of course it is." Young boys had flitted in and out of my life for twelve years while I tried to cram History and English into them. Everything in their lives—from the frogs in the pond at Roger Williams Park, to the size of their peanut butter and preserves sandwich—was important.

He tugged me over to the pews in front of St. Catherine's statue. "You did good finding those killers and getting those kids out of trouble. Nonno said you were a real good detective, and that you knew about things better than most of the cops."

"Well, I suppose that's because people trust nuns and tell

them what they wouldn't tell the police or anyone else. I just listened really carefully, put two and two together and was lucky to figure it out."

"Yeah. But it must have been fun, too, finding out all that stuff."

"No. It wasn't fun, Dante. It was really sad most of the time. But it was necessary."

"What I wanted to ask you . . . this is . . . this is sad but necessary, too."

"All right." I raised his head with my index finger and wasn't surprised that he was on the verge of tears. "What do you want me to do?"

"Find out what happened to my mother." He sniffed and wiped his nose. "I'm worried that someone killed her and might want to kill my dad, too. I don't want anything to happen to him. Please. You can do it, can't you?"

CHAPTER TWO

Great God! Give me wisdom. Give me courage. Give me a break from so much heartache!

With gentle and intermittent prodding from the Lord, I found the words that calmed this hurting boy's heart. We talked for a while, Dante and I, and I prayed that what I said would be enough to reassure him—if only for a short time. As we talked, two men and a lovely, well-dressed woman walked through the rear of the small lady-chapel on their way out the side door leading to the area where the altar boys' changing room was. Her heels *clack*ed on the marble floor, echoing noisily. Only a few minutes into the Mass and she was fleeing already? *Yes, Lord, I know. That wasn't charitable. I will do penance this evening. The rosary I promised four months ago will be sufficient? Then I had best start on it while we sit here a bit.*

A door clanged as one of the men left the nave proper, probably to use the restroom Father Lawton had installed recently in an unused closet. The smartly dressed woman smiled and waved to Dante and he smiled back.

"She's pretty, isn't she?" he asked thoughtfully, and his inflection let me know that he truly wished an answer to his question.

"Very."

"Uncle Carlo says she's the spitting image of my mother."

"He does, does he?" So who was she? "So, who is she?"

"Aunt Rachel. Mommy's sister."

Ah, that explained his careful scrutiny. "You miss her dreadfully, don't you? Your mother, I mean."

Dante curled into my side, holding very still, then sighed. "I guess I do. But I'm starting to forget what she sounded like. You know, her voice." He sniffed. "I guess that means I'm starting not to remember her. It's awful, not being able to remember."

Oh, dear God, help this child! What do you mean, you want me to do it?! But . . . Okay, Lord, no buts. Do unto others. I get it. Thou proclaimest. I obeyest.

Dante wiped his nose with his hand and I fished in my voluminous pocket for a clean handkerchief and held it out to him. He blew and curled once more into my side.

So this was what it felt like, this warmth tucked near my heart, this small child with complete trust, this mothering that I had never truly felt until right now, for this motherless child. I probably should have had some Gospel quotations to tell him, or some platitudes that always begin, *it will be all right.* But it wasn't all right. For him, it would never be all right again. He thought now that he was forgetting; but floods of memories would crop up later in his life to haunt him.

Smells were the most vexing things. I could remember exactly how my father smelled—the apple wood smoke that streamed out of the potbellied stove at his lots, the heady scent of the grapes he crushed with his Italian friends, the wine they bottled. Not always his voice, but definitely his scent; and when something came close to that, a huge shudder undulated through my entire body. It was the best experience, and the worst. How could I explain to Dante those horrible moments of love, loneliness and loss? *Not charitable nor possible, Father.* So I protected him with my strength as best I could, and he soon quietly settled.

But my insides were not settled, and I wondered how much time needed to go by until they were. Not only for what I had promised Dante at the beginning of our talk, or the recognition of the loss in my own life, but also, alas, because of what I shouldn't feel for this boy, but did. Perhaps I truly was the worst of nuns.

Our small moment of contemplation was interrupted much too soon by an impeccably dressed, blond, mustached, tall and slender man. A man who had been my horrible, mean childhood nemesis who had actually—no lie—dunked my braids into an inkwell at school and—bloody, beastly boy—had glued the ends together one day while I was sleeping on the edge of the surf at Oakland Beach. I got a haircut I didn't deserve that night. Told him I would forever hate him, but didn't tell him that I liked the short bob better. The bloody, beastly boy had turned into the handsome, loyal man I would forever call friend. Richard DelVecchio slid into the pew behind us and ruffled his charge's head.

"So this is where you got to." At Richard's deeply timbered, slightly mocking voice, Dante jerked away from me and scampered over the back of the seat, fairly launching himself at Richard. "Whoa!" Richard said. "Remember where you are. Hear that bell? Monsignor Grace is about to distribute communion, and your father will expect you to receive."

"Okay." Dante stole a glance at the candle we had lit in front of St. Catherine's statue. "Richard, Sister Agnes promised to . . ."

Oh, good grief, Richard was going to kill me! "Dante, not now," I said. "You must go back to receive communion. We'll talk later."

Richard pointed Dante in the right direction, gave him a little shove and a pat on the small of his back, and then he turned to me. "Vincent will expect you at the farm for the usual reception."

"I can't go . . ."

Dante jerked to a halt and turned. "But everyone's going to

be there. You have to come. Besides . . ." He jammed his hands into his pockets and shifted his gaze to the candle we had lit. ". . . that's where it happened."

Before I could close my mouth, Dante was gone. He was gone, but Richard lingered, his eyes slit and determined, his shoulders and body tight. Uh-oh. I'd seen that concentration many times when he was trying to whack the daylights out of a tiny ball in his silly golf games. Right now it appeared that I was the ball, and he was about to whack *me*. Should I duck, or merely bluster my way through? Nope; bluster wasn't going to do it. Ah, well. In for a penny . . .

"Not now, Richard. Communion first."

"You won't get off that easily, *Sister* Agnes. I'll let it go for now because I'm not about to make a scene at this Memorial Mass. But don't think for a minute that I don't know what you're up to. Dante's been hinting at it for days." He let me precede him to join the line of communicants at the altar rail. I knelt. He knelt. And then, horrors of horrors, he leaned over and smiled, dangerously. "We're not finished, Aggie," he whispered. "Not by a long shot."

He'd timed it perfectly, because the altar boy stuck the gold paten under my chin and I had to stretch out my tongue to receive the host from Monsignor Grace, making it impossible to retort. Men!

Less than a half hour later, after Vincent Ricci had invited all the nuns to his reception—and I wondered if Richard had arranged that—we were waiting at the curb for several of Vincent's vehicles, which were to take us to the farm. A familiar maroon-trimmed, ivory-colored Cord brougham glided to a stop in front of Winnie and me, and Richard leaned over to open the door.

Oh, no. He wasn't going to trap me inside that thing. "We'll wait and go with Mother Frances in the big Ford touring car," I said.

"Not this time, Aggie. We have to talk."

"Richard . . ."

"Don't make a scene, *Sister* Agnes. Do you really want Mother Frances to know what you're planning?"

Winnie opened the back door and popped into the slightly smaller rear seat so I would have to sit in front. Before I was comfortably seated, she poked me between my shoulder blades. Hard. "What are you planning now, Aggie?"

"Nothing much."

Richard snorted. "Nothing much, my as . . ."

"Richard!"

". . . pidistra. Go on. Tell her or I will."

Before Winnie could pounce, I protested, "It's not my fault."

"Hah! It never is," she said.

"Dante just asked me to help him out, that's all."

Richard slammed his hand on the steering wheel. "That's the biggest damned lie you've told in many moons, Aggie. And to your best friend, too." His head swiveled slightly to catch Winnie's gaze. "Dante told me she's going to investigate Catherine Ricci's death."

Winnie choked and had to cough into her sleeve before she could speak, and then it came out in small puffs of outrage. "You didn't! Didn't you have enough? I can't believe what you're planning to do." She pulled out her rosary and began to pray, the beads *click*ing together to the sound of the motor.

"It was pitiful," I said to them both, "the things he said to me and the way he said them." Though Winnie was probably concentrating on her prayers, those bat ears of hers would ensure that she'd hear everything. "The boy's hurting. He's confused and angry and he thinks everyone has failed him."

"Have you forgotten that this isn't part of your calling?" Richard asked. "As you so often remind me, you are a nun!"

He didn't say *not a detective,* but I knew it was on the tip of his tongue. "Would you refuse that boy anything, Richard? Besides, I'm probably not going to discover a single thing. The police have already investigated, haven't they? If there was something to find . . . if Catherine's accident was more than an accident, they'd know it, wouldn't they?"

He looked at me as if I had two heads. "Since when are the police interested in helping Vincent? All they want to do is put him behind bars. If they could do that by investigating his wife's death, they'd do it. If not, they aren't going to waste their time on anything this petty. Damn them."

I could have reminded him that he had just received communion, but I knew his unwarranted arrest and three-day stay in jail three months ago was incentive enough to cause this bitterness. "What did Dante mean when he said that the farm was the place where it happened? I thought his mother died in an auto accident."

"She was at the farm. Behind the wheel of a car that had crashed into a tree. So it looked as if she were driving it."

"And she wasn't?"

"I honest to God don't know." He sighed. "I was giving her lessons every week, and she was eager to learn. She listened carefully and practiced using the brakes and shift."

"I have no idea what that is."

Richard frowned. "It's impossible to demonstrate with this car. The Cord has a front wheel drive, not like the farm's Ford. This car has a shift right here on the dash." He touched a horizontal lever. "Here's the shift, but in the Ford it's a knob on a shaft that sticks out of the floor. Each shift is different, but each one goes from one level of gear to another to increase the speed of the car. There's a pedal on the floor that puts the car into a neutral drive so the gears can change."

"Too much information," I said. "I'm a visual person. I have to see it."

"Okay. I'll show you after everyone leaves the reception."

"I'll hold you to that."

"So," Winnie said, abandoning her beads for a moment, "what's the gear ratio?"

"She knows about cars?" Richard asked.

"Anything scientific, she knows it. I still think electricity is magic. She knows voltage and amps, whatever they are."

Winnie said, "Voltage is . . ."

I knew if I didn't stop her that we'd be wallowing in scientific terms the entire trip to the farm. "Never mind! I prefer magic."

Winnie *humph*ed. "You're my greatest disappointment. All these years with me and you still don't know simple physics." She leaned over and pointed to a few instruments on the dash. "Here's a fourth-grade explanation. All those dials and levers have to mesh together in order for the gas to get to the engine, for air to mix with the gas, and for the engine to work the gears that make the tires go round. And the driver has to know how to do what, at the precise time when it's needed. And this, my dear Agnes, is not magic, just good physics."

She sat back with a satisfied smirk. She was entitled. Science—physics, botany, chemistry, biology—was her specialty, and she knew it. "Thank you for that, but I'll still need a demonstration."

"Right," Richard said.

"So, if Catherine had learned without your help, then she could have been driving the car. Which reminds me . . . you said you would give me lessons."

"Don't change the subject."

"Just reminding you."

"I haven't forgotten. I had to make sure I had enough life insurance before I let you get behind the wheel. If you drive as well as you cook, the whole danged state had better stay off the roads." Suddenly, he swerved the car over to the side of the steeply winding hill and stopped it with a limb- and torso-jarring jerk. "I don't know . . . *was* she driving? She shouldn't have been driving. What was it she said during that last lesson?" He banged his head on the wheel. "God damn it!" Bang with his head again. "What a dimwit! If you hadn't got us started on this I wouldn't have any doubts. But now . . ." He lifted his head and grabbed my cheeks. "I could kiss you."

"Richard!"

Bang. Bang. Bang. Only this time the banging came from my side window.

"Open this door! And get your hands off her!"

Richard scowled, but dropped his hands. When I saw who was making such a fuss, I rolled down my window to glare at my one-year-younger cousin, a newly promoted sergeant in the Providence police force. The one who had stupidly arrested and jailed Richard during my first investigation of a crime—a multiple murder—and then been given much of the credit for solving it, hence his promotion. Now here he was again.

"Have you been following us, Josiah?"

"Of course he's been following us," Richard said. "The police always follow Vincent and his—um—employees. I'll bet they were salivating at the people who were in attendance at Catherine's memorial." He muttered under his breath, "Couldn't solve her death any more than I could." He began pounding on the steering wheel again. "Damn! Damn! Damn!"

Winnie's beads kept on *click*ing, only much faster.

"What is wrong with you?" I asked Richard.

"You!"

Winnie's beads stopped clicking. "Could have bet on that one." Then they started up even faster. Was there a marathon going on back there? Would she get extra points with God if she finished her prayers faster than the speed of light?

"Your interference. Your insistence on not being a good,

ordinary nun. You get me mad, Aggie."

"Yeah," Josiah said, "the whole family understands that. Hell, the whole damned state!"

"Will you men stop swearing? I don't even know what I did."

Richard ran his fingers through his thick mane of hair. "You got me thinking, Aggie."

"And, as we all know, *that's* tantamount to breaking a commandment!"

"Aggie!"

"Okay. Sorry."

"I was picturing you behind the wheel of a car, driving on the back roads on the farm."

Josiah doubled over, laughing. "Aggie? Driving? Are you kidding me?"

"That's just it. That's what convinced me. This clodhopper of a woman behind the wheel of a car."

"The saints preserve us," Josiah said with a quick sign of the cross.

"Except, now that I think about it, Aggie's not really klutzy," Richard said.

"Are you nuts?" Josiah asked. "She almost burned down her mother's kitchen."

"I was there. But that's not klutzy. When she's bored, she has a problem concentrating. Her wood fires roar out of control. Her soups burn. Her needle pricks her fingers. Her straight stitching goes all crooked. And her iron leaves big brown marks on the cloth. That's because she's always thinking of something else instead of concentrating on what she considers the boring task at hand. But when she's holding a gun and pointing at a target, she can hit dead center every time."

Aghast reaction from Josiah.

"Shut your mouth, cousin," I said.

His lips wobbled, and finally he sputtered, turning his attention away from me and addressing Richard. "Aggie can shoot?"

"Yeah. She's probably better than you are. I know she's better than I am." Richard pointed towards me. "Look at her. She's smiling and her eyes are flashing with excitement. She loves to shoot. Probably wishes she had more chances. I ought to get Vincent to put her on the payroll."

"Hey, Sarge!" someone shouted. "The captain wants to know what's holding this up!"

Josiah waved him off with an *in a minute* gesture, and then turned back to Richard. "What's this all leading to?"

"I'm not sure," Richard said, "but I'm beginning to think there was no way Catherine Ricci was driving that car I found her in."

He found Catherine? Oh, dear God!

He stared through the windscreen, into the distance, and the expression on his face made my heart ache. He was in pain. Not physical pain, but, perhaps, spiritual. Or emotional. I thought for just a short minute that he might scream. But he shook that off and a worse expression took over. His face hardened and his eyes glinted with pure, unadulterated hate. He looked as if he could kill someone.

"It's taken me a whole wasted year and then an interfering, confounding, impossible, wonderful nun butts in, and now I'm almost sure that Catherine Ricci's accident was no accident. And if it wasn't an accident, and she wasn't the type to kill herself, and she *wasn't,* then there is no other explanation except . . . murder."

CHAPTER THREE

"You pulling my chain?" Josiah asked. Richard just glared at him. Icy. Furious. After a couple of seconds, Josiah nodded. "Okay. I'll take your word for it. But I'm not sure my captain will." He squared his shoulders and took a deep breath. "Be right back." He slapped his hand on the hood of the Cord. "Stay here!"

Normally, Richard would have retaliated for that slap to his precious Cord. But he didn't react at all. What was he thinking? Why had he sat there, with only that furious glare for Josiah? I thought about that look on his face when he'd mentioned finding Catherine's body. That bleak look, filled with anguish and guilt. And perhaps one other thing?

Had he loved her, his employer's wife? Is that why he'd never married, never even had a long-time girlfriend? Had he pined for Catherine Ricci over the years and had to watch her every day with Vincent, a man whom those loyal to him both loved and feared, and others despised? Someday I was going to prod him about Catherine. Now wasn't the time, however. But the very thought that I might be right made me very uneasy. Why hadn't he said anything? He had always been my best childhood friend, yet I'd never until this moment thought he had a secret this huge. *Jumping to conclusions, Father? Maybe you're right. Okay, okay. You see into our hearts. You would know. So, tell me, is it true?*

His refusal to answer such a simple question spoke—as they

say—volumes.

In contrast, Josiah's return was a brass band compared to Richard's sober silence. Well, a pursed-lips band, actually. Was that "Yankee Doodle Dandy" he was whistling? What was making him so happy? Oh, wait! Another coup, of course! He was in on a hot lead. He was Johnny-on-the-spot once again, and if he discovered what had really happened to Catherine, his career would go up another giant step. And he'd ingratiate himself with Vincent and the Ricci family. That couldn't hurt.

Josiah walked his fingers over Richard's car, opened the little door in the back and scrunched his large body next to Winnie's. "Okay, the captain wants me to follow up, so let's go," he said, slipping his notepad out of his pocket and licking the tip of his pencil. Why did men do that? It made no sense. Wet leads don't write; they tear paper. Besides, they taste terrible, like stale beer.

"You're coming with us?"

"The captain says that since I know all of you, riding with you will speed things up. So, yes, I'm coming with you." He wrote something on his notepad, probably the date. "Let's have your suspicions, DelVecchio. And I'll look into them."

"Sure you will. I've been on the wrong end of your suspicions, Sergeant Morgan. I don't especially like your methods."

"Look, I was fresh out of the academy, all bluster and brawn and not enough brains, ya know? I listened to the wrong guys at headquarters, who had—pardon the expression—a vendetta against anyone connected with Vincent Ricci. And, yes, I wanted to make a big arrest. But in the end, I got tangled in my own ambition and ended up totally wrong about you. Just help me out now, okay? I won't let you down."

Richard couldn't have been more surprised than I was. "Just don't touch my car again," he growled, "and we'll be okay."

"Gotcha!" Pencil poised over his notepad, he prompted, "So

31

what's going on? Why murder?"

"Because she wouldn't have been driving that car."

"How do you know?"

"She gave up."

"So it was suicide."

"No! She gave up trying to learn how to drive."

"Now you're contradicting the report. It says she was driving."

"And a different report three months ago said I was guilty." Richard wound down the side window and signaled a turn. Was a crooked elbow *left* or *right?* Right! As he wound it back up, he craned his neck to look through the smaller back window and said, "I'll try to explain. After several lessons from me, she knew how to drive. She just couldn't do it."

"She knew how to drive and she didn't know how to drive. That doesn't make sense."

"Yes, it does," Winnie said. "Knowing how to do something and being able to do it are not the same." I heard her tapping at something and turned to see her poking her finger on the slightly wet page of Josiah's notebook. "Write this down," she said. "If I'm correct about what Richard's telling us, she had no problem understanding how the car worked, she just had a problem with the mechanics of working it herself."

Richard answered, "Good logic, Sister Win. And you're right. Look, Josiah, in simple English, she couldn't get the shift and gas pedal down pat. She tried as hard as anyone could have, but she stalled the engine every damned time. See, *she* was the clumsy one, not Aggie." He smiled, then frowned, then shook his head as if trying to clear it. "All this talk about Aggie and teaching her to drive zipped something into my brain that had been buried a long time. Catherine liked to be perfect. She had a perfect life—"

"With Vincent and his lot?"

"You wouldn't understand. She grew up with us. She knew what was going on. She knew she'd have a life of luxury, and if it was one thing that Catherine liked, it was what money could buy. But that's not what's important. What was important to Catherine was her idea of perfection. She was blond, but not blond enough, so one night when everyone was sleeping, she sneaked down to the kitchen and poured peroxide on her head. Screamed bloody blue murder, almost burned her scalp off and the house reeked for days. She was thin, but not thin enough, so she forced herself to throw up after every meal except dinner, when Vincent was there. She was poised and graceful, but not enough, so she took dozens of dance lessons and kept tripping over her feet or stomping on mine. She couldn't even master a simple box step! And then there were modeling lessons, but the books fell over every time she had to balance them on her head, and she couldn't get that swingy walk right. She looked like a prancing goose; but I couldn't laugh at her or she would have gone stony silent for days. The only lessons she came close to perfecting were the etiquette lessons, and then she mixed up the forks or her flower arrangements collapsed. It was one thing after another—all just to be perfect. But she wasn't perfect, and unlike Aggie, she was furious when she couldn't do something."

"What do you mean, unlike me?"

"You do something I really admire. You don't give up. You keep trying, even if you hate what you're doing, like singing at High Mass this morning."

"But you laughed at me!"

"Sure. That sound that came out of your mouth was hilarious. But you didn't turn and run just because you couldn't make your vocal chords do what they needed to do. That's really brave and admirable."

The only response I could make came with a great rush of heat that must have scorched my cheeks.

But suddenly something niggled at my brain, something similar to Catherine, and then I had it. "Oh!" I turned to Josiah. "Catherine was just like Cousin Lonnie."

"Lonnie? But that's sports, not flowers or dances," Josiah said.

"And sports are more important than what Richard just explained?" At his quizzical expression, I sighed. "If Lonnie can't make a perfect basket, he walks off the court. If the football slips out of his hand, he walks off the field, mad as a wet cat. And it takes months for you and the rest of the cousins to wheedle him into another game."

"Yeah? So?"

"Picture it. What if Lonnie couldn't learn how to drive?"

"No big deal. He'd just bum rides from everybody."

"Catherine didn't have to bum rides. She had Richard or another of Vincent's men to take her anywhere she wanted to go."

"Lucky me," Richard said. "But that meant she had to hide her latest failure from Vincent. And that's the last conversation I had with her. After stalling the car at least a dozen times, she begged me to tell Vincent that she was doing just fine, but she wasn't. I told her I couldn't lie to him, so I guess she did."

"According to the report of the accident," Josiah said, "Vincent said she usually practiced on the farm, and we have two collaborating statements to back him up."

"That's probably what she told him and everyone else. He never asked me—and nobody else did—so I didn't have to lie. And we never talked about it. He loved her. He put up with her mood swings, and he never questioned her dropping one thing for another. If she said she was practicing, he'd believe her, even when he shouldn't have."

We turned onto New Hope Drive in Scituate and up to a white shingled guard house next to heavy woods. Everything we could see was surrounded by a tall, spiked iron fence. The guard waved at Richard and hurried to open a set of huge iron gates. "Everyone else is around back," he told Richard. "Vincent said to park in your usual spot."

"Thanks, Dom."

"This is a *farm?!*"

The long oak- and spruce-lined driveway branched at the foot of a steep rise. One road looped in front of a house that perched on the top of that rise. The structure was long and low, not the usual New England Cape Cod style, nor the familiar Victorian that the newly rich had built all over the state. This looked as if it had grown right out of the land itself. Rock and brick and stone combined with dark wood in a wonderful harmony with the land around it. The lush trees brushed the deep overhang of the roof and, although there was symmetry to the landscaping, it looked almost primitive. Wildflowers predominated, with heather and mint crawling blissfully over sun-dappled and shady areas.

"I've never seen anything like this," I said.

"It's called Prairie Style," Richard said. "Some guy in Chicago designed it. The inside is as good as the out. I'm sure Vincent won't mind if I show it to you later."

Richard followed the bend to the right and drew up under a portico. He helped Winnie and me out of the Cord, and watched, grinning, as Josiah bent himself like a Swiss Army knife to get out of the back. The four of us ambled down wooden walkways to the back gardens where three white tents had been erected for the reception. I smelled sausage and peppers, the rich tang of perfect pasta gravy, and meat roasting.

"Herman gave his life for this party," Richard said.

"You killed a cow?"

"A steer, Aggie. Boy, you really don't know science stuff. Cows give milk. They're too valuable to eat. But we have about fifty chickens for eggs and another fifty or so for food. Then there are the rabbits, pigs and sheep, and seven horses and ponies to ride. We grow corn, wheat, pumpkins and squash, tomatoes and green beans, an acre of gourmet Italian vegetables, a vineyard and orchard, and Christmas trees."

"This is a real farm!"

"Don't sound so surprised. It's the Depression, and Vincent's food donations help several organizations feed the really needy. And that reminds me . . . Vincent has another donation of beef for the convent. I'll have it delivered tonight. It's not as tender as the last batch, so you'll probably want to actually make soup out of it for that soup line of yours."

"Don't tell *her*," Winnie said. "Other than that night you sneaked into the convent and helped her with the stew, she's not allowed to actually cook."

I leveled a freezing glare at my best companion, who had the good manners to give me a level gaze instead of another caustic remark. She was right, however. I couldn't make edible food. But Richard was right, too. I really didn't pay attention. I didn't like to cook. Ergo, the food came out god-awful. *Sorry, Lord; but you know it's true.* "I'll pass along your message to Sister Noble, our new novice, who's a whiz in the kitchen."

The next half hour was a blend of rich food and a blur of familiar faces and the notorious. Monsignor Grace offered a blessing on the food and several uniformed waiters served lasagna, small beef steaks, roasted chicken, several salads, and plenty of dark, pungent red wine. Different factions gathered together, but each table had at least one nun at it. Smart. Vincent knew there were tensions, and easily diffused them.

The family table was filled with people I didn't know, and two children—Dante and a cute little blond child, who kept herself glued to the side of the pretty lady from the church. Her mother? Who else? Interesting that she had flaunted the usual old country funeral attire for something more . . . I could only call it rebellious, but lovely. She and her daughter wore coordinating outfits. Envy—mine—reared its ugly head. Here I sat, straight pins that held on my headpiece poking into my scalp, while the woman—Aunt Rachel, Dante had called her—sported a lovely little red straw. It had a small, rather rakish feather tucked into the red-and-white-striped ribbon trimming. When she escorted her daughter into the main house, probably to use the facilities, her figure wasn't hidden by a slightly itchy tent like my garment, but a perfectly tailored soft white coat. The matching dress had a long, full skirt sprinkled with tiny embroidered red, white and green flowers. The little girl wore a sweet pinafore of the same fabric, topped by a green knit sweater, lace-trimmed white ankle socks and shiny white shoes. But Rachel's footwear was outrageous high-heeled platform shoes.

Red shoes!

I looked down at my own old brogans poking themselves out from under my black serge skirt. They were black and clunky with tight black laces that confined and pinched, not soft and red with holes cut in the side and front so feet could breathe and toes wiggle. What would it be like to walk on those hardly there stilts? How would it be to walk without encumbrances like the rope cincture at my waist, holding in place a hot skirt that wrapped itself around my ankles and tripped me up way too often? I might be a nun, but I could appreciate the lovely and more comfortable things in life. I might even covet them. All right, I did covet them, but that was only occasionally and never in preference to what I wore as the Bride of Christ. I was heartily, definitely, decidedly happy I had chosen the church. Most of the time. Except those were really spiffy-looking shoes.

After the meal, I looked around for Dante, and Richard noticed. He guided Winnie and me over to a small copse of trees nearest the horse barn. Five yipping puppies poked their heads out of the barn door, rolling like tired tops, cuddly and pudgy.

"Look up," he said.

I had to search through the branches, but then I saw it. A tree house, painted green and brown, with splashes of buff and yellow.

"We had a bunch of paint left over and he commandeered it."

I didn't know if he was trying to achieve it, but Dante had created a young boy's idea of camouflage. "It's delightful. How do you get up there?"

"Ladder nailed to the back of the tree."

I strode away before he could stop me, but he caught up much too quickly. "Darn your long legs."

"You are not going up there!"

"Why ever not?"

"Monsignor Grace. Mother Frances. The reporters from the *Providence Journal*. And a few cops watching through binoculars."

"Darn my socks!"

Josiah ambled up, a plate of clams casino in his hand. "I'd like to take a look at that accident scene, if you don't mind."

"Haven't you seen the photos?"

"Yeah, but they're no substitute for the real thing."

"Okay. But I better tell Vincent. Be right back."

I waited until he was too far to stop me, and then glided up to the side of the tree. The ladder looked sturdy enough, but to be sure, I tested it by hanging from one of the rungs with my full weight. Perfect. "Dante? Want some company?"

He opened a small window and hung his head out. When he caught sight of us, he grinned. "Just you?"

"And me, too," Winnie said, handing Josiah her glass of iced coffee. We grinned at each other—it was an adventure—and hitched up our skirts, tucking them into our rope cinctures. She chuckled. "Hope those reporters didn't bring photographers with them. Wouldn't this make a great front page?"

"Richard will have a fit if he sees us."

"Then let's make sure he doesn't see us."

The ascent was fairly easy. I only slipped once, when I tried to get my frame inside a doorway meant for a small boy.

"It's easier if you sorta back in," Dante said. "On your, um, bottom."

"You're right. It is easier."

Winnie and I wiggled our way into the interior and found that we couldn't stand upright, so we plopped onto the floor, sitting Indian-style in the middle of the room. A larger version of the puppies—but one that was much, much cleaner—crawled onto my lap and licked my cheeks. "What's his name?"

"Pal."

"Is he yours?"

"Not really. I have a dog back at the house named Caesar. Dad *says* he's my dog, but when we're here at the farm he's mostly with Dad. This one is mostly with me."

The little house was delightful for a young boy. He had chairs and a table and walls covered with *National Geographic* photos of African animals. A bookcase stored comic books, some lead soldiers, and a couple of trucks. Mostly, however, there were piles of books in every corner in upturned tomato boxes. Lucky the tree house was built as sturdily as an ordinary house or I'd have boxed up those books and put them in a safer place.

"This is great. Cozy."

"The best part is the view," he said, pointing to one wall that was mostly window. "I can see loads of animals and birds from here."

"I have to see that." Careful not to bump my head, I went

closer to the window. "This is breathtaking. Winnie, come see!" She and I opened the double window and stuck our heads out. The air held the scent of wild honeysuckle, funky fungus, and pungent pine. The vista included hills and valleys, a small apple orchard, some corn fields displaying the first shoots of green, brindled cows feeding on green grass, and myriad one-lane roads meandering in and out of the woods. Mostly, however, way in the distance was the sparkling water of the Providence reservoir—its inlets, its tiny islands close to the shore, spots of movement—maybe ducks and geese?—on its surface. I could imagine deer and raccoons in the verdant darkness, waiting for dusk to prowl for food and come down to the shore to drink.

"I wish I had a camera," Winnie said. "It must be wonderful, seeing this every day."

"You think they have places like that in heaven?" Dante asked.

"I'm sure of it," I said. "Maybe even better."

"Good. Mommy should be in a place like that."

If hearts could break, mine was rupturing. This was another hidey hole for a boy who made one wherever he went, even in the basement of St. Catherine's Academy. I wondered if his father knew how lonely Dante was. It was about time someone told him. *Right, Lord?*

"Aggie, get down here or Josiah and I will go without you!"

"Party pooper," I muttered and Dante chuckled. "Can we come back some other time?"

"Sure. But if you're going to stay, you've gotta bring a blanket. It gets cold at night."

When we were settled in the battered Ford that Richard had borrowed, I jumped down his throat without hesitation. Someone had to. "Does he sleep in that tree house?"

"Sometimes."

"Alone?"

40

"Sure. What's wrong, Aggie? You look like you just sucked a lemon."

"Huh! No nine-year-old boy should be out in a tree house all night by himself. It's not safe."

Josiah laughed. "Are you kidding? This is Vincent Ricci's kid. He couldn't be any safer."

"I'll bet that's what Catherine thought, right up to the minute of her death. Here. On Vincent Ricci's safe farm."

Chapter Four

We drove in total silence as each, I imagined, struggled as I did with what I'd just said. The sun still shone and the birds still sang. God was in His heaven but all was not right with the world, for gloom had settled all around us. So I wasn't paying much attention to where we were going, except that we left the manicured part of the farm and ended up amongst heavy woods. Finally, I could stand the silence no longer. Patience is *not* my middle name.

"The implications are staggering, of course."

"What implications," Josiah asked.

With a snort and a roll of his eyes, Richard retorted, "What Aggie means is that if Catherine was murdered, then it had to be by someone we know."

"Why? Because there's a gate, a guard and those iron spikes? You guys might not realize it, but we've scaled that fence more than once." At Winnie's shocked intake of breath, Josiah looked abashed, and a mite nervous, like a rabbit in a flashlight's beam, but he blustered his way through, not realizing that he was just digging a ditch for himself. "Not often. Just when there seems to be something cooking. And I don't mean food."

"We know what you mean. We've had to live with the constant harassment, even when we didn't deserve it," Richard said. "Guess Vincent was right. We do need armed guards patrolling the perimeter."

If I let them continue, we'd be here arguing for eternity.

"Enough, both of you. We have more important things to do than hurl accusations. We must get to the bottom of this, and the first step is realizing that no matter what we discover, the truth—as the greatest philosopher said—will hurt. In more ways than one."

"Oh, there she goes again," Winnie said, clicking her rosary like a toy skeleton. "Don't get her started on that Plato stuff. We'll never hear the end of it."

I tried to zip a quelling look over the back of the seat, but Winnie knew me too well and turned so it missed its mark. As if that could stop me! She believed in science. I believed in another kind of truth. "Some day I'm going to have enough nickels to buy copies of the *Allegory of the Cave* for every child in the upper grades. It should be mandatory for every American. Maybe we wouldn't all be so blind."

Winnie groaned. "Too late. Once she gets started you need to have earplugs on hand!"

"Well, it's true. We don't see what's right in front of our eyes, so we all jump to conclusions before we know the facts, and we accept things for truth that have no foundation, only hot air and gossip. Witness the assumptions Josiah makes all the time. Just because Vincent appears to be a gangster doesn't mean he is."

"And it doesn't mean he isn't, either," Josiah retorted.

"But you and everyone else in Rhode Island will never know for certain because you take surface and suspicion for reality. To get to the reality, you need to look below the surface into the heart of the matter."

"I leave it up to the Almighty to do that," Josiah said. "I've got my own bailiwick to keep in order."

Richard stopped abruptly at the top of a sloping hill.

"Here?" I asked.

He nodded, staring at a large copse of massive oaks and spruce, with a sprinkling of chestnuts and maples struggling for a foothold. Wild roses twined their way up the trunks and over fallen logs, poison ivy keeping them company. Robins and blue birds flitted high in the branches of the trees, probably bringing insects to fledglings in safely hidden nests. It was hard to imagine that death had visited this peaceful place. I scanned the area of forest at the bottom of the hill, finding what I hoped I wouldn't—a jagged healing scar on two of the oaks, as if they had been chewed by a monster. A murdering monster, in this case?

Winnie walked around the crest of the hill, then began to descend, heading straight for the scarred trees. Stones shot out from under her and she stumbled, but righted herself before she fell. "Has anyone driven down here since the incident?"

"Not that I know of," Richard replied. "Why?"

"I think we should test it," Winnie said.

Josiah stomped his way over to her, but didn't descend the disintegrating slope. "Test what?"

He needed a good smack on the back of his head. Why were men so dense? I would have jumped down his throat, but Winnie patiently answered, "Test whether the car could have rolled down this incline all by itself so that it built up enough force on its descent that it would result in the tragedy your lot thinks occurred. Or whether it was necessary to push it into the trees to obtain the same result."

I could see Josiah's indecision. *Lord, give us a break, could you? The man is slow to know. Step in. Whisper in his ear. Warn him of the hounds of hell, but get him to move. Please?!* The Lord had his ears tuned to us, thank goodness, because Josiah nodded.

"You got a car you want to sacrifice, Richard? Maybe that lemon of yours?"

"It might come close to a pale yellow, Josiah, but it's not a lemon. And, by the way, it cost more than your year's salary. It won't be the Cord that gets sacrificed. But I think I can find

44

some clunker in the barn."

"It should be the same size and weight as the car Catherine was in. The same model will be best," Winnie said.

"Shouldn't be a problem. Vincent bought a fleet of them. You want to do it now?"

"No time like the present."

While Richard went to fetch the car, Josiah took my elbow to help me over a small rock, as if I were some kind of invalid. I'd just climbed a ladder to the skies, for crying out loud! I shook off his hand and scrambled over the uneven ground all by myself. It took more time than I expected because the shale on the hill shifted at each step. Of course I stepped the wrong way a couple of times, but the high tops of my sturdy, unflattering brogans kept my ankle fairly steady. I only twisted it once—a fitting punishment for my stubbornness with my closest cousin. Josiah did help Winnie around the crest of the hill to a safer descent. Finally we were at the bottom, and Josiah looked back up to where we'd started. How in the world were we going to get back?

"I don't see what this is all about," he complained.

"Do you believe what Richard says?" I asked.

"Not without proof."

"That's what this exercise is all about."

"And you're going to prove it? How?"

"Not me. Winnie?"

She went to the point of impact—if that's what it was. "Speed and incline," she said, ruminating aloud as she usually did. "Or, incline and speed. Or possibly point of impact."

We were at the trees, and she bent slightly to trace the outline of the gouges.

"One is at my knees, but the other is almost six inches higher. How is that possible? If the gouges were made by the same automobile, then shouldn't they be at exactly the same height?

45

Yes," she said emphatically. "But these are not. In fact, they look as if they had been chopped out of the tree with an axe, not a round bumper or headlamps." She glared at Josiah, a glare that could have frozen an Eskimo, but Josiah squared his shoulders. He was playing cop again. Heaven help us. Winnie prodded, "You didn't notice this?"

He looked at Winnie as if she had two heads. "For crying out loud, it's been a whole year. The stupid trees grew, one of them faster than the other."

"Of course they did." Winnie had that cat-toying-with-a-mouse look. "The only problem with what you're suggesting is that it's scientifically impossible."

"What? Trees don't grow?"

"They grow. The trunks get more girth and add rings for each year of their growth. But a tree doesn't grow from the bottom up. It actually grows from the top up. So the gouges should each be at the same height they were last year. And if they were uneven like this last year, then all your lot is blind as hedgehogs." She shook her head and bit her lip, her usual movements when she was trying to solve a difficult problem for her class. Why not here? Why not now? "There's something very wrong. I'm not sure exactly what it is yet, but I should know once I see the car."

While each of us was puzzling out the scientific—or any—implications of what she'd just said, Richard returned. Behind him was a brand-spanking-new and much larger car than the one we had arrived in. It pulled up right behind the old battered Ford that Richard got out of. "We're down here," I said.

"Be right there."

"Careful. There's lots of shale and it gives way easily."

Richard waited for the driver of the other car who exited his car in one lithe motion. He stood there a moment, lit a thin black stogie cigar and blew pungent smoke high above his head.

He was a tall, muscular man in a three-piece grey suit with a very thin navy pinstripe. On his head was a cocked grey fedora. The two of them maneuvered their way over the boulders and shale; and when they got to where we were, Richard introduced the large man with the bulbous nose and cleft chin as Pietro DiSilva. He had grey eyes. I'd never seen an Italian with grey eyes. I wondered if he had chosen his suit on purpose to compliment his eyes. If he had, he must have known the effect it would cause, one of confidence and trust.

He doffed his hat and smiled. "Call me Tiny, Sisters. Everyone does." He cast a sneering look at Josiah while speaking in a much more cultured voice than his pugnacious body and face suggested he would. "Well, bless my soul, what do we have here? A man in blue, late to the scene as usual. But we shouldn't complain, should we, Richard? We've waited long, and Vincent and his son have suffered much, but finally someone is getting to the bottom of this year-old mystery."

After Winnie explained what we'd found, she turned toward Richard and Josiah and asked, "I wonder . . . did the police find any glass in those gouges?"

Josiah frowned. "Glass?"

"I just can't figure out if the headlamps broke during the crash or if only the bumpers hit the trees."

"There was no glass on the ground or on the hood of the car," Richard said.

"That's true," Tiny agreed. "When I arrived I looked over everything carefully. There was no glass broken. The headlamps were intact, as was the windscreen."

"I wish we had photos," I said, "so we could check all this out."

We all looked at Josiah. "There are two at the station house, but it would take hours to get them over here."

"Ah, perhaps I could help," Tiny said. "I, uh, took a few shots with my Brownie. I'm an amateur photographer, but have won some awards for my work. The accident photos are not up to my artistic standards, but they do show the scene accurately. I have them in my darkroom files. When you finish up here, I'll drive you up to the back gardens. Vincent will be serving coffee and pastries soon. He wishes you all to attend him. I could bring the photos there."

Winnie was standing transfixed, looking up at the automobile that Richard had driven to the top of the hill. Three times she looked from it to the damaged trees. Her brows shot up, and she sighed and shook her head. She swiveled to look at the trees again, and then turned back once more to the car, looking intently at something that had her furrowing her forehead. What the heck had caused that reaction?

"Winnie?"

"Richard," she said slowly, as if weighing each word for its full implication, "is that vehicle exactly like the one Catherine was found in?"

"Yes. Vincent bought four of them."

"Josiah, what were Catherine's injuries?"

"I was still in the academy when it happened," Josiah said. "I've only read the reports."

"I can answer that," Richard said. His gaze refused to land on any one of us as he seemed to shrivel in on himself, remembering. "There was a huge smashed-in place on her forehead where her skull had been crushed, and another smaller dent on the back of her head. There was also a lot of blood. That's how she died. Bleeding to death in the front seat of the car."

"No other injuries?"

"The report said there were severe broken bones in her legs and arms," Josiah offered, adding, "The cops assigned to the case figured she smashed the car into the trees, and the impact sent her into the windscreen, where her skull was broken. Then she probably was thrown backward and hit something else hard. The bones could have been broken by the shift or the steering wheel shaft. At least, that's what was in the report."

Winnie took three steps up the hill, slipped and staggered. Tiny ran to help her. "Sister, you should not attempt such a strenuous ascent. Take my hand."

When they arrived at the top, she walked to the car that was like Catherine's death trap. Her hand ran over the bumper and she stood immobile, looking first at the headlamps, then at the trees, and then covering her eyes and bowing her head. It was as if she were trying to visualize what had happened—or praying for guidance.

Help her, Father. This is very important. I'm sorry, Lord. I should have realized you knew that already.

"Richard, help me up the hill," I ordered. When I arrived next to Winnie, I touched her shoulder and she snapped out of her concentration. "You know, don't you?" She nodded and there was a bleak resignation that set her lips in a tight line and shadowed her eyes with sorrow and anger. "Tell us."

She sighed. "I'm no expert; but you don't need an expert to see what happened—not if you look carefully. You don't even need to reenact the accident." She pointed to the copse of trees. "There are two sets of gouges. One comes to my knees. The other, about six inches higher." She stood next to the car and pointed to the headlamps. "I'm a tall woman, but so is this Ford. How old is it, Richard?"

"About five years."

"The reconstituted Model T?"

"Yep."

"Stripped, like my father's, or with everything on it?"

"Stripped, except for the automatic starter. We don't need more than the basics for the farm."

"I thought not, but that doesn't matter just yet. Right now, just a glance will tell you that the front bumper sticks out about five inches in front of the headlamps. So the bumpers would be the first point of impact. But unless the car had been traveling at great speed and got launched into the air, a car like this couldn't hit the trees where those gouges made it look like it did. The bumper is much lower than the lowest scar. And the highest scar is much lower than the headlamps."

Tiny ran his hand over the headlamps and bent to the front bumper. "Will you stand next to the car, Sister?"

"Certainly."

He measured with his hand held slightly away from Winnie. "You said one of the gouges came to your knees." She nodded. "Uh . . . I don't mean to be personal, Sister, but where would that be?"

Oh, bother it! That's what happens when you wear tents for skirts. Winnie stuck her knee out so there was a decided bump at the front of her skirt. We could all see that neither the bumper nor the headlamps lined up with that bump. And if the other gouge was six inches higher, then that should make it at the middle of her thigh.

Josiah said it for all of us. "They don't match."

"No, they don't," she said, pushing past me to open the passenger door of the car—the only door in the front that could actually open. She inched her way across the coarsely upholstered bench seat and settled in the middle. "If Catherine hit anything—anything at all—she would have been jerked backward at first, then flown forward, as Josiah said. But if she had been driving, the steering wheel would have hit her dead in the center of her chest. I imagine that could do a lot of damage, maybe even kill her, but it certainly wouldn't have given her that head wound. However, if—as the police said—she was driving, and she was going very fast, she *might* have been jostled enough to fall across this seat. I don't think that's what happened because you really . . ." She twisted and jerked, trying to move toward the middle. It took a whole lot of twisting and jerking. ". . . can't move easily against this upholstery. That's one thing out of whack. The most important thing, however, is that in a car like this—a *stripped* car like this, where there are no latches for the front windscreen—she would not have hit it hard enough to crush her skull, because . . ." Winnie put her hand out and pushed rather gently ". . . *this* would have happened." Not even a bird chirped as we all watched the windscreen swing out on its two-way hinge.

"Holy Mother of God," Josiah said.

"If she had hit anything, she would have gone right through this and landed on the hood of the car, where she would have slid into the tree. She would never have hit the back of her head on something hard in the car because the seats are upholstered. Although she might have broken her legs and arms, they would have broken because she hit something outside the car. She would never have died inside the front seat. In fact, Richard could never have found her *in* the car at all unless someone put her there." When she turned to look at us, a lone tear coursed down her cheek and anger darkened her eyes and burned her cheeks. "There is no doubt in my mind that she was murdered. The only question is *how.*"

"How?" Richard paced back and forth, kicking at rocks in his way, clenching and unclenching his fists. "I should think the most important question is *who.*"

"Again, I'm no expert, but I think if we can figure out the how, we might be able to discover the who."

"I don't like to contradict any of you," I said. "But I truly think the how will come last. First comes the who, then comes the why, then comes the how."

Tiny put his beefy hand on Richard's shoulder. "My friend,

we have a hard task ahead of us. We must tell Vincent."

What they didn't say, but what I knew they were thinking because I was thinking it, too, was that as soon as Vincent heard the news, he would want to tear up earth and heaven to discover the truth. If Vincent was old school, vendetta was all he knew. God help the murderer. In cold fact, God help us all.

CHAPTER FIVE

Tiny offered to drive so we could leave the other car there in case Vincent wished to examine Winnie's deductions for himself. Tiny's auto was a large Lincoln brougham the kind rich people had where a chauffeur sat in front and the passengers had nothing but comfort in the back. It accommodated us comfortably, and he settled Winnie and me in the front seat, putting soft squabs behind our heads that were similar to the ones my Newport friend, Mrs. Vandergelder, had in her limousine. From his impeccable wardrobe to his impeccable automobile, it was easy to see that Pietro "Tiny" DiSilva appreciated—and could afford—the very best in life.

"You might be more comfortable in the rumble seat," he said to Josiah, who scowled and climbed into the back with Richard to gentle laughter from our new acquaintance. "Only joking with the man in blue. Since I don't have servants, I switched out the rumble seat for a luggage compartment."

We stopped at the tree house, but Dante wasn't there.

"He'll be at the house," Tiny said. "He never misses dessert. Vincent's cooks are the best."

Although I was still reeling from the complications that would result from Winnie's deductions, I couldn't help myself. I had always been intrigued by the way the other half lived, so here was my chance. "Cooks? Plural?"

Tiny smiled. "Two distant cousins, imported all the way from Italy."

"My goodness! Why?"

"Ah, nostalgia," he said. "It gets the better of all of us. Don—Vincent's father, Donato—lived here at the farm until his lungs gave out; and he comes back as often as his doctors will let him. Many times he told us that he dreamed about the tastes of his village. As he's been corresponding with his family since the turn of the century, it made sense to him and Vincent to help two deserving widows and give Don one final taste of home. They were delighted to come. Who isn't delighted to come to this country? Wait until you taste their desserts. Their zuppa inglese and cannoli . . ." He kissed his fingertips in that age-old Italian gesture that shows approval. "*Molto buono!* The culmination of their culinary skills. Of course," he added, "there are two highly respected chefs who are paid well to cater to occasions such as today's and an in-house scullery maid to do the cleaning for the old ones. But mostly it's just family."

Richard chuckled. "Family? Yeah, you could call it that. But family means something entirely different to Italians than to your lot, Aggie. When we're here at the farm it's not unusual for twenty people to be here for supper. Or breakfast, for that matter."

"This is true, Sisters," Tiny said. "You do not have to be related by blood to be considered family to Italians. Business acquaintances, neighbors and visitors of all kinds may be included in that description. And then there are those who merely drop by to pay respects."

"Lord have mercy! Twenty people? This is normal?"

"What's wrong, Aggie?" Richard asked.

I could hardly speak. What had I gotten myself into? When Dante asked me to help, I knew I'd get some opposition—*All right, Lord, a lot of opposition*—from Mother Frances when she found out what I was doing. And she would find out. There was nothing that went on in the convent that could be hidden from her for very long—and that included Richard's nefarious gift to me three months ago. But I had decided to chance being able to hide this investigation from her, thinking it would be only a matter of asking a few questions, and then finding out that Catherine's death truly was an accident. Now . . .

"Josiah knows what's wrong," I said. "Twenty people here at the farm means twenty suspects just in the immediate area. Sorting all that out will be a huge job for anyone."

Especially me. Darn my socks! I had had evil in my life before—like the murder of that poor girl on church grounds and five others we discovered later—but this was different. The murderers then were truly warped, but ordinary. This was Vincent Ricci. There was nothing ordinary about him, his organization, his ethics, his friends, his enemies, and his power. I had the sinking feeling that before this was finished, I was going to owe a hundred rosaries to God, to add to the year's worth that was already my debt from past escapades.

A nun wasn't supposed to have escapades. Or tiny little pearl-handled pistols that she hid from a very suspicious and very astute Reverend Mother. *What was in your mind, Lord, when you bade me to be a nun? Were you just waking from a long nap and couldn't get your thoughts together? Was this the lesson of the century or a cosmic joke? Take my word for it; don't quit your day job. Abbot and Costello, you aren't. No, I am not even slightly amused. Nor is Mother Frances. It's not easy being the non-nun nun. And worse being her Mother Superior.*

Josiah leaned over the seat back, resting his head on top of his hands as he looked out the windshield. "This is a sorry mess, Aggie. If you count family and friends, or business associates and enemies, we're dealing with a platoon. But if someone breached the fence like the force has, you're talking a battalion as suspects."

"More than that," Richard said. "If you count anyone who

has business on the farm, you've got a small army, because the regular farm workers alone add another dozen to your battalion. We have seven men and four women here every day doing physical labor, some in the house and some on the grounds, and we import workers during plowing season and later in the fall to harvest the crops."

I looked up, in my mind's eye piercing the roof of the car all the way to the clouds above our heads, and beyond. "Don't go away. We're going to need you."

"Sweet angels and saints, there she goes again," Winnie said. "If it isn't Plato, it's God. The only difference is, prayer isn't enough. She actually *talks* to the Almighty."

We'd had this conversation a thousand times. When Winnie prayed, they were the Church-sanctioned prayers. Our Fathers. Hail Marys. I had a different system. "He always listens and he always answers prayers, right? Then prayer is just like a telephone call. When you pick up the receiver, you expect someone to answer and talk to you. So, I just call Him and He answers. And why shouldn't He? He's ever present. I don't know how it works. I just know this is the right way for me to keep in touch with Him. Besides, in a case like this, we're going to need all the help He can give."

"This is one hell of a day," Richard said.

Since I agreed with him, I didn't admonish him for his swearing. Hell was involved, all right. But as long as we stuck together, and had a little help from the mansions in the clouds, we'd get through it. *So stick around a little longer, please, Lord. We've got Vincent to contend with.*

What would his reaction be to our discoveries? I'd soon find out, and for the first time since I'd met Dante's father, I wasn't sure he wouldn't pursue this with guns blazing. Heaven help everyone in Rhode Island if that happened. The state hadn't had a true vendetta in more than a decade. But this—

Catherine's murder—was more than reason enough to start one. Of course, there was never a good reason for anything like that; but we were dealing with centuries of tradition, and an underground justice system that was ruled by blood feuds, retribution, and family solidarity turned upside down.

As soon as we pulled up under the portico, a line of departing cars was just turning down the driveway, and another car was pulled up to the front of the house, its passengers waiting inside. Josiah excused himself to hurry to the coffee. The only people left on the portico were Dante, Vincent, Monsignor Grace and Mother Frances. Bother it! No way to hide what we'd been doing, and no way to exclude her. Darn my socks! We all waited until the last of the sedans drove away, filled with four of the sisters.

Sister Justina waved to us and settled herself in the front seat, smiling to beat the band. She was the oldest of the order and deserved pride of place—and a little comfort and . . . there was no other word for it . . . fun. She had had little of that in her seventy-three years, sixty of them spent in the order of the Merciful Sisters of Mercy. I wondered if we were ever again going to know what fun was—or if we were ever going to have any fun ourselves.

I would have to start facing pain and sorrow as soon as I told Dante what we'd discovered. Yes, I would have to tell him. It was his request of me, and he deserved to know the results from me. But how much did he need to know, and how in the world do you tell a little boy that his mother had been murdered and half the state was implicated?

Implications! I was beginning to hate that word. Would it rule the rest of my life, or just this weekend, or this month? What if I couldn't help solve the murder? What if no one could? Would the world erupt in violence in the attempt to uncover the truth? Right now, there was a smiling Vincent Gaetano Ricci walking toward the house after the final car drove off, his large hand engulfing the small one of his son. I took a gulp of air for courage and followed closely behind.

Richard took my elbow, while Tiny offered one of his arms to Winnie and the other to Mother Frances. It was obvious that she was surprised, but she made no fuss, although she kept a slight distance between her and the big, smiling man who smelled like tobacco and bay rum.

"Let me handle this," Richard said.

"You handle Vincent. I'll talk to Dante."

"Don't you think Vincent will want to do that himself?"

"Yes, and I'd love to turn this over to his father, but I'm not sure I should. After all, Dante asked me, personally, to look into his mother's death. I think he will want to hear what we found from me or from Vincent and me—or even from you, Vincent and me. When all is said and done, he's going to need everyone to help him get through the tough days ahead."

"Then wait until I tell Vincent."

I nodded and watched as he whispered to Tiny, who easily handed Winnie and Mother Frances off to another of Vincent's associates. Smooth. Very smooth. As if discussing murder was normal routine for these men, necessary perhaps. The same smooth handoff occurred with Dante, and this time the boy ended up with Tiny while Richard opened a side door, waited for Vincent to enter and, after a solemn smile to me, closed it behind them.

I hurried and caught up with Dante and Tiny just as they rounded a corner onto a large patio surrounded by raised beds of kitchen herbs, roses and wildly colorful annuals and perennials. I loved gardens and wished we had one at the convent. Well, we did have one, of sorts—a sorry little patch that Sister Justina tended; but her cataracts were blinding and she often mistook weeds for asparagus. She deserved the pleasure this small task gave her; but if I were very, very good perhaps I could take over when she could no longer make the trip out to the backyard. The thought tickled me, as did the pungent smell of black coffee, anisette and orange skins blended with the sweetness of hazelnut and almond oils.

Yes, my mouth watered. And my eyes rounded at the mounds of whipped cream and the platters of jam-filled bars or sugar-dusted fried cookies. What was that sound? White-coated waiters worked a complicated machine that poured out milk foam onto coffee served in tall crystal glasses with handles on them. It had been almost three hours since we'd eaten the main portion of the meal, so I followed Monsignor Grace's lead and dug into the creamy pudding of the zuppa inglese and a crisp-fried fruit and cheese cannoli. Tiny was right. Superb. I only hoped they and the anisette-laced coffee would give me the courage to face the smallest victim I had ever known.

Josiah joined us, and we went to sit in comfortable chairs grouped around a table at which sat Monsignor Grace, Mother Frances, and the lovely woman from the church and her little girl. "Hello," I said to the blond, blue-eyed cherub. "And what's your name?"

She smiled shyly. "Ellen."

Dante loped over and balanced on the arm of my chair. "She's my cousin. And this is Aunt Rachel." He pointed to a small group of people who were talking quietly on the other side of the patio. "That tall man with the grey hair and round glasses is Uncle Mark, Daddy's accountant."

"My husband, Mark Branch," Rachel said. "The rest of the men are Vincent's associates and friends."

"I'm Sister Agnes, this is Sister Winifred, and this is my cousin Josiah Morgan."

"I already knew who you were," Rachel said, laughing. Although she glanced at Josiah's blue uniform with badge, she didn't seem surprised and included him in her conversation. Good manners, I thought. "Dante talks about you all the time, Sister Agnes. According to him, you're the best thing to come along since sliced bread."

She said it with friendship and I smiled at her. She took a silver cigarette case out of her pocket and chose one of the longest cigarettes I'd ever seen, holding it up. As if on cue, Tiny leaned down to light it for her. She blew a stream of smoke into the sky and lounged back into the capacious chair. "We all followed your escapades with that murdering bunch. Good work, all of you."

"Thank you."

Monsignor Grace waved a waiter over for a refill of his coffee. "You've been busy today, too, Sister Agnes. We've missed your sparkling conversation. Nothing amiss, I trust?"

A rush of fear coursed through me. I didn't know how much to tell the monsignor, not before I had permission from Vincent. And I certainly couldn't answer here, with everyone so close, especially when we didn't know the *who* or *what* yet. Why, judging from this motley crew, it could be any of them. A quick flush swept through me and I glanced at Mother Frances, who was watching us closely.

"Well," Monsignor Grace said after a thorough sizing up of what must have been my startled and wary face, "I shouldn't worry. If you're involved, everything will work itself out satisfactorily." He tipped up his glass and took a long swallow. "I must also commend you for your contribution to this morning's Mass." He leaned over and patted the back of my hand. "It was a valiant try, and I thank you for accommodating me."

"You're most welcome, Your Eminence. But I beg that you won't feel inspired to request anything like it any time soon."

He laughed, and his eyes crinkled like the newest cinema

heartthrob, Clark Gable. "I don't think there's any fear of that, Sister. Once may be enough for a lifetime."

As I was reaching for a fourth cannoli, Tiny leaned down and moved the plate more than an arm's distance away, whispering, "Vincent wishes you to join him and Richard in the library. Just go through the door Richard took."

"Aren't you coming?"

"He wishes to see you first, then the rest of your clerics."

"I'm not a cleric, just a nun."

"You're not *just* anything, Sister Agnes. You are one of a kind."

Oh, my stars, that was kind of him. But it wasn't true. I was one of a million nuns, each with her own talents. It's just that no one really notices any differences, thinking the sameness of our habits hid a sameness underneath.

I knocked when I got to the door and it opened quickly and quietly. A lovely elderly woman dressed in black with a bibbed white apron smiled and bowed her head slightly, and I was sure this was one of the imported cooks. I wondered if she could teach the clueless to cook. *"Andiamo."* She smiled and waved me to follow her. She might be able to teach, but for me to learn, I'd have to take Italian lessons. I knew a few words but not enough to keep up with the way Italians talk—all speed and hands. Maybe Richard would teach me Italian along with my driving lessons—if I ever got them.

She might be old, but she was certainly spry. It wasn't easy to keep up with her. Especially in the loveliness that beckoned to me in the short hall. It was lined with rich oak panels and molding, and there was the scent of lemon oil and wax, which were probably responsible for giving the wood a sumptuous gleam. The oak floor was covered by a plush Turkey rug in reds, mostly. Marble-topped tables held an occasional piece of delicate pottery as well as large vases filled with roses and heather. The lamps were electric, not the lanterns or oil lamps I had grown up with, and the glow from them turned what could have been a dark tunnel into a striking, well-lit gallery.

Yes, gallery. Oil paintings graced each wall in Impressionist riches. Was that a Monet? A Seurat? Oh, sweet honesty! One after the other, frames contained dots and splashes and great brush strokes of landscapes and interiors and portraits. I was gawking, but what else was one to do when faced with this treasure? I wished I had time to do more than just catch a glimpse of the life that filled this small space. I wondered who had planned this, who had known this much joy. If it had been Catherine, as I suspected, then Vincent had lost so much, he would be . . .

Pacing. Richard put his hand out and I halted as Vincent prowled round and round the room, from one corner of a huge slab of wood that served as a desk, to a spot behind a long, three-cushion sofa, to the window overlooking a rose garden, to a large portrait of a woman who looked like Dante's Aunt Rachel. Catherine Ricci had been beautiful, for sure; but the artist had captured something more than merely her beauty. There was also a haunted quality about her. Was that the truth of this woman, or a stylistic addition? From all that Richard had said, I thought it was more substance than style. This woman on the wall was lost, and perhaps she knew it. How awful that must have been.

Vincent paused in front of the portrait, and then spun, looking around as if he, too, was lost. This large, powerful man's gaze couldn't fasten on one thing in this library, three walls of which were covered with book-filled shelves from floor to ceiling. He gave a deep growl of frustration and took up pacing again, clenching his hands together as if they contained someone's neck. His hair, which had been neat, clean and in place only minutes before, now looked as if someone had raked up leaves in it. He stopped to take me in and there was so much anger and, yes, hate in his eyes, that I stumbled to a halt.

"What Richard told me . . . is this real?" he asked.

I nodded.

"God damn it to hell." He flung himself into a large leather chair, leaned back and covered his eyes with his forearm. "I have enemies. Not Catherine. Me. Not my wife. Not the mother of my son. Just me. She must have been mistaken for me. No one would hurt her deliberately. It's just not possible."

"Yet it happened," I said.

If this man was who they said he was, he was used to barbarism of the kind that had come to his own door, and I had no patience with his it-couldn't-have-happened attitude. He had to come to grips with the truth, and quickly.

"Vincent, I hate to say this, but you leave me no choice. Catherine could not have been mistaken for you. Look at that portrait. She was slender and yet her form was definitely that of a woman. She was found in broad daylight, so it wasn't dark when she was murdered. And you know better than anyone what was done to her. Those injuries could not have been delivered by mistake. Someone deliberately caved in her skull— with terrible force in the front and less in the back. Whoever it was broke her legs and arms—before he killed her or after, I don't know. What I do know is that he then set up a phony accident scene to fool everyone. It worked. It might have worked forever if your son didn't love his mother so much that he demanded to know just how she died. What are you going to tell him?"

CHAPTER SIX

Vincent Ricci's head snapped up and he began to rise from his chair. "Do you know who you're talking to?"

Lucky for me, a nun's habit hid everything from torn undergarments to shaking knees. Mine. I grasped the large rosary tucked into the cincture at my waist and lifted it to dangle the crucifix between us. My family had given the rosary to me on my tenth anniversary as a nun. It was fashioned from zebra wood and sterling, with tiny onyx beads for the nail heads and etched ivory as the scroll, spelling out *INRI*. It was intricate and lovely, and made to be heavy enough to constantly remind me who I was and to whom I belonged: INRI, Jesus of Nazareth, King of the Jews.

"I know who I'm talking to. Do you?"

He stopped, staring at me. The fire in his eyes didn't abate all that much, but I didn't expect it to. His pain and anger were much too raw.

"You have courage," he said. "More than a lot of people I know. Perhaps it comes from this."

He reached for the crucifix and held it in his hand, running his thumb over the nails in Christ's feet. I wondered if he was praying. I wondered if he remembered how. He let it fall from his grasp and it swung back into place at my right side, clunking against what was hidden there.

"What was that?" he asked.

"What was what?" I avoided looking at him and Richard, trying to appear innocent and nonchalant, and knew that I was failing miserably. Although I sometimes hid things I was feeling—some kind of self-protection, I imagined—I really didn't know how to use outward subterfuge with others.

"Wait a minute," Richard said, scrutinizing my eyes, which were gazing at a spot a little to the left of nowhere as I sucked on my lower lip. If I looked evasive, he looked dumbfounded—a fairly normal expression when he was with me. I don't know why. "You can't look at me."

"Yes, I can," I disagreed, but couldn't force myself to shift my gaze to him. "Oh, bother it!"

"I don't believe it. You don't really have it with you, do you?"

Darn my socks! He didn't have to be so perceptive right now! "Where else would I have it? It's not something I can leave lying around where anyone could find it. Like Mother Frances or some new sister who doesn't know the rules."

"What are you two talking about?"

"Richard's gift to me during my last problem with murder." I pulled out a flannel bag holding the silk-covered box that housed my most notorious gift. I had double-sewn the bag, but it was still more than a bit lopsided. "He thought I needed protection." I tossed it to my friend, who caught it in midair. "I love your gift, Richard, but, please . . . a nun with a gun?"

"Is it loaded?"

I dug in my valise-sized pockets and held my hand out to reveal five bullets, coated with a white substance. "I think I lost one."

"Is this face powder?"

"Chalk."

"I need to sit down."

"Richard, now I know what attracts you to this interesting woman," Vincent said, smiling for the first time since I'd arrived. "Things will never be predictable with her around."

Wait a minute! Attract? Interesting? Me? He had to be kidding!

"You need to put that away before our other guests arrive," he directed Richard.

"I don't have pockets as big as hers!" he said, shooting me the same exasperated look he'd used when we were kids. It didn't work then, and it wasn't working now—although I did feel the urge to stick my tongue out at him.

Vincent shook his head and went to one of the bookcases. He reached in, fiddled with a book, and a loud click sounded just before a small section of false-fronted books swung out to reveal a hidden safe. Richard handed him the bag and bullets, and he laid them beside a mound of money, so much money that I couldn't breathe for a moment. He shut the book door and sat behind his desk.

"You are one of the most intriguing people I've ever met," he said to me. "No wonder Dante loves you and Richard thinks you walk on water."

"And I love *Dante*," I said, glaring at my so-called friend, who was still shaking his head with exasperation and more than a little disbelief. "So what are we going to do about this dilemma?"

"I'm used to making decisions about my son, just not this kind."

"He needs to know."

"Yes. But before I tell him anything, we need to understand what we're dealing with. Is your cousin still here?" When I nodded, he picked up the telephone on his desk and listened a moment, then spoke Italian into the mouthpiece before laying the receiver back into its cradle. I had only understood one word—*monsignore*. "They'll be here shortly," he said to Richard. "Meanwhile, tell Anna that we'll need ice and other fixings for drinks."

After Richard left, Vincent motioned for me to take the chair he'd vacated. I was grateful to sit so my nerves would quit twitching. "Do you have any idea who would do this?" I asked.

"To Catherine? None."

"What about someone you know absolutely *couldn't* have done it."

"In my world, anybody is capable of anything."

"So that's why everyone isn't in here being told what happened?" He nodded. "You live in a dangerous world, then. Although recently I found out that my world isn't immune, either. Or anybody else's world, for that matter."

A soft knock sounded, and Vincent said, *"Entrare."* Even I could understand that Italian word. The lovely older woman opened the door wide enough for Josiah to enter. *"Grazie,* Anna." He waited until the door closed before he acknowledged Josiah. Did he think Anna might be a suspect, or, as with the others, was he merely being cautious? "Have a seat, Sergeant Morgan," he finally said, "and tell me what you're going to do now that you know that my wife was murdered."

"It's not up to me," Josiah said. "Never was. She died on this farm, which isn't in Providence. So if anyone is going to investigate, it would probably be the state police, because Scituate has a very small force. I think only two part-time officers. But I am going to recommend that someone do a complete investigation."

"Way too late for that, don't you think? There's no murder scene, because some police officer—state or local—decided it wasn't one. There are the trees, but you already know what they prove. But there's no car because I junked it, hating the reminder sitting around this place every day, not wanting my son to have to see the vehicle where his mother died. So what can you do? What can any of you *really* do, that would make a difference?"

"Police can only do their best."

"Over the years, I've had experience with your best, and that's not good enough. No, not nearly good enough."

The door opened, and Richard and Tiny ushered in Monsignor Grace, Mother Frances, and Winnie. Right behind them, Anna wheeled in a trolley holding a plate of cut-up lemons and limes, a sugar bowl, napkins, and a bucket of ice chips. I watched Vincent scrutinize each person in turn, concentrating, assessing them as they talked, as they moved, as they paid attention or didn't pay attention to what Anna and Tiny were doing. What did he think about Josiah positioning himself against the wall, eschewing a chair, primed for just about anything? Or Mother Frances choosing the chair farthest from the others and not saying a single word after ordering her drink, only picking up her rosary to say a quick decade? Or Monsignor Grace lounging in the largest chair, scooping a handful of peanuts out of a nearby wooden bowl, and crossing his legs—such a departure from his usual role? And Winnie, who surveyed the room and moved a small club chair close enough to talk quietly to me if we got the chance?

Interesting, the mix of people that resulted in this invitation. Were they what he expected, or wanted? But the most important question, for me, was: why had Vincent gathered them together following the most devastating revelation he'd ever received?

No one seemed to notice his rapt but stone-faced attention. They were more interested in Tiny, who removed his rakish hat, went to the bookcase on the wall next to the desk and opened a section to reveal a well-stocked bar. Richard asked for drink orders from all of us, and it was interesting to note what each one requested. Winnie and I were as predictable as toast, asking for a fruity wine. Richard opened a bottle of Asti spumante, pouring us each a generous flute of the sweet Italian version of champagne, while Tiny mixed a bourbon and water for Richard, a nice manly drink. Monsignor Grace ordered, "Scotch, neat." His heritage or a penchant for that strong, smoky taste? Mother Frances surprised me a bit when she asked for a whiskey sour; but her request for two cubes of sugar in it didn't surprise at all. She could contend that it was merely a slightly different kind of lemonade.

Tiny sweetened her drink and then took four cubes out of the sugar bowl and put them on a napkin. Irish whiskey on ice for Josiah was his normal drink. He also ate green potatoes and drank green beer on St. Patrick's Day. Heritage! Got us every time. It tickled me that Tiny would mix himself a martini with an onion. But maybe that wasn't so unusual. He was a classy guy, and this was a new, classy drink. The only real surprise was that Vincent didn't order a drink at all. Instead, Tiny poured him water over ice with lemon and lime squeezed into it and handed him the napkin with the sugar cubes on it. Tiny's service to Vincent was so automatic that I had to assume that this powerful man didn't drink—perhaps to keep his wits about him when others were losing theirs.

I set down my wine when a plaintive whine and scratching erupted outside the door. Tiny opened it and a dog entered, trotted right over to Vincent and immediately sat on his haunches. "Good boy, Caesar," Vincent said, and tossed him a sugar cube. He caught it in midair and swallowed it whole, then stood on his hind legs, dancing in a circle. "All right, but this is the last one." The dog seemed to know what Vincent said because as soon as he got his second treat, he went to the hall door and Richard let him out. That exchange was a glimpse into another side of Vincent—a man who loved his son and his dog, even though he was probably exactly what the police suspected. Humans were an interesting experiment. Did I say that God wasn't as good as Abbot and Costello? He wasn't. He was better—at least with macabre humor.

"Now," Vincent said to all of us, "let me tell you why I asked you to join me here in my office."

As he solemnly outlined the events of that day, Mother Frances glared at me as if it was my fault. Well, she had blamed the other murder on me, why not this one? It was curious and vexing to her—and me—that I stumbled on these events. Was I being tested? *Or is this a gift from you, Lord—perhaps a way to magnify my calling? I'm going to have to find out for myself? Why not? Inscrutable, your ways are. Or is that Charlie Chan? Sorry. As you know, my mind wanders, even in a situation where I need to pay attention. Silly of me. Are you sure I wasn't meant to be a blonde?* Well, it didn't matter. My hair was so covered up that no one knew it was deep, dark mahogany and very curly, like my mother's.

Mothers. Dante. *Lord, the boy has such grief waiting for him. Thankfully, he doesn't know it yet. Give him a few more hours of being a little boy, a few more dreams instead of nightmares.*

My attention snapped back to the murmurings around me when Monsignor Grace said, "You have my condolences."

"Thank you, but I need more than that," Vincent said.

"Whatever is in my power, you have it."

"I need, from all of you, complete silence about this discovery. Treat it as if it were a confessional. Not one whisper." He smacked the desktop. "Not one!" His jaw tightened along with his fist. His eyes were lit with a fire that was frightening, and it was readily apparent that he was fighting some inner demon. He banked that fire quickly. But a banked fire could easily flare to life, and if that happened, I couldn't imagine anything less than a conflagration resulting.

Josiah leaned forward and fixed Vincent with a baffled look. He opened his mouth, and got a *"What the hell?"* out, but Mother Frances took that moment to speak for the first time. "You can hardly make demands, Mr. Ricci," she said.

Without looking at her, Monsignor Grace raised his hand. "I think in this instance, he has the right." He did not smile at Vincent, but he nodded with all the authority of his rank and privilege. "Sergeant Morgan, what would happen if this information got out? Wouldn't it be plastered all over the front page of the *Journal*?"

"Sure, but what difference would that make?"

"Well, it would alert whoever did this. But, more important, it just might start an internecine war. That is what you're trying to avoid, isn't it, Vincent?"

"Got it in one, Robert. My business is such that I have enemies . . . well-hidden enemies, as we now know. I need time to find out who they are. My way. Without the police. Without interference from reporters or scandal mongers."

"But if we give you our promise to keep this quiet," the monsignor said, "what assurances will you give that this won't erupt into that war?"

"If a war erupts, it will not come from me. You have my word on that."

"Is that all you want us to do, keep silent?"

"Not by a long shot. There's much more I need from each of you if we're going to find out what happened to my wife."

"You can't hold me to that," Josiah said. "I have to report to my captain. What am I supposed to tell him?"

Men! Give them a uniform and a badge and they think they have power over the multitudes.

"You could tell him that you attended a Memorial Mass and met most of the Ricci family," I said. "And you could remind him that now that you have a nodding acquaintance with Mr. Ricci, you could probably get access none of his other officers have. That could give you some importance in the squad and keep him off your back. And who knows? You might actually solve this murder. I'm sure, then, Mr. Ricci will hand the murderer over to the police so Dante at least would get some justice out of all this horror."

"Are you sure she's a nun?" Vincent said to Richard. "She sounds more like a lawyer." He looked at me with a hint of a smile. "You could be Secretary of State. That was one round-about way of putting pressure on me."

"Well, you promised no war. I just want to ensure that justice will be served."

"My family has been here since 1888, and they haven't seen justice in all that time."

"Perhaps not. But in this instance, shouldn't an example be laid down for Dante? Or do you really want him to learn about vendetta at his young age?"

"You don't play fair."

"I wasn't aware this was a game. Nor, at the end, was Catherine."

"Low blow, Sister."

"Not at all. Eye for eye and tooth for tooth is Old Testament. With Christ we live under a new covenant, and we are admonished to seek justice, not revenge. It's part of his teachings in that *Love thy neighbor* commandment."

"*Basta!*"

I looked to Richard.

"It means *enough,*" he said.

This time, Vincent pointed his finger at me. Whoops! I suppose I *had* gone too far.

"I gave my word not to start a mess that could put everyone in danger," he said. "But I can't speak for the lunatic who did this. He murdered a completely innocent and trusting woman. Someone I loved more than . . ." He waved away whatever he was going to say, but it was obvious that his emotions were right under the surface of his anger. "Killing someone who never hurt anyone in her life makes me more uneasy than you know. In my business, any trouble is always business related. Always. Anyone who knows me knows this. Taking out my wife isn't business. It's personal or it's warped beyond simple understanding. I need time to find out whether it's personal or warped. I need help to . . ."

Terrified screams echoed from outside the hall door, and Vincent jumped to his feet. He jerked his head to Tiny, who put his hand in his pocket and dashed from the room. Considering what had been in my pocket only minutes before, I had a suspicion the big man wasn't looking for his handkerchief.

CHAPTER SEVEN

We practically crashed into Tiny at the door to the kitchen, but he quickly stepped aside and then went to the back door, blocking it with his height and bulk. As I had feared, we came face-to-face with my third encounter with pure evil.

A young girl pawed at the air and clutched at the front of her modest grey dress. There was spittle on her lips, which were curved into a grotesque grimace, and some vomit leaked onto her bodice. I ran to her side, but before I could help her she jerked backward with great force before she toppled and lay at my feet, her body sprawled half on and half off the chair she had just overturned.

"Winnie!" We tried to lift her but Josiah stepped in to feel for a pulse. He looked up and shook his head. "God have mercy."

She was so very young, perhaps no more than twenty. She looked uncorseted, yet wore tiny pearl earrings stuck into her lobes and a small pearl and gold cross on a long gold chain. Her blond hair was pulled back into a bun covered with a delicately crocheted net. Her hands . . . one was clutched around the table cloth, her last act as she fell. The other was still at her bodice, where she had torn several buttons out of their holes. Her nails were clipped in a rounded arc. They were shiny, but not polished. She was obviously working as a maid or kitchen helper, but from her jewelry and the way she took care of her nails, I wondered if that's what she truly was.

Most of all, I wondered *who* she was.

Before I could voice my bewilderment at the incongruities I was seeing, Vincent went to a screaming Anna and helped her to a chair in the corner next to the Hoosier cupboard. A stream of Italian, punctuated by great sobs, accompanied Anna's gesticulations. I wished I understood what she was saying, but the only words I could make out were *Ella,* obviously a first name, and *impotente,* and I knew the Latin root for that: help-less. Anna had felt helpless while it was happening, while the girl was dying. So had I. So had we all.

Vincent said something about Ella, patted Anna's shoulder and went to Richard. "Where's Carlo?"

"Went back to his room after lunch."

Vincent picked up the receiver of a wall telephone and dialed seven. "Carlo, didn't you hear the screaming? No, it wasn't the pigs." He rubbed his neck and stretched. "There's been some trouble in the kitchen, and I'll need you down here. Check on Ella first. Anna said she went upstairs over an hour ago to take a nap." He replaced the receiver. When he saw me watching him, he arched his back. "Pure tension." He looked over at Anna, who had quieted down but was now crying into her handkerchief. "I was just making sure my cousin Ella is okay. She's much older than Anna and always lies down in the afternoon."

"And Carlo is . . . ?"

"My brother. He came home from college two days ago, dragged some of his junk up here and has been unpacking it almost nonstop." He surveyed the large, modern kitchen and the dead girl smack in the middle of it, and sighed. "I suppose the police should be called."

"No need. Josiah's lot is probably still parked outside. Send someone to get them."

"You always know what to do, don't you?"

"Not according to Mother Frances."

"She doesn't know what she has."

Once more he enlisted Richard's aid, and he went in search of someone to fetch the other cops. He didn't have far to go. The rest of the family arrived all together. Tiny kept all the others at arm's length but allowed Rachel one quick look. I thought she'd scream or do something most silly women do, but she only made a small sound and quickly blocked Ellen's and Dante's way. "Uncle Vincent and the other grownups have everything well in hand, kids. Let's go ride the ponies."

"But you said we couldn't, that I would mess up my new dress," Ellen said.

"Changed my mind. You can wear Dante's clothes."

"Boy's clothes? Mom!"

"Unless, of course, you don't want to ride."

"No," Ellen protested. "We do! We do!" She hopped on one foot, then the other, with a grin that showed missing teeth, excited at the thought of the horses.

Rachel's backward glance showed her concern, but she was a mother, doing what mothers did, gathering her chicks and taking them to safety. Richard said something to Rachel's husband Mark and he loped down the hill to the parking area, got in a small roadster and headed to the front gate. If I knew Josiah's men the way I knew Josiah, the police would be here quicker than Vincent would want them to. And since I did know them from the last deaths I'd investigated, I also knew they'd stomp their way in and shoo us all out, asserting their dominance, eschewing our help. *Dear Lord, save me from male stupidity! Well, I'm not really sure you* are *male. If you are, you're a very different kind from the one you invented for this earth.*

The other men backed off, sitting close to the house and waiting for orders, I supposed. Or did they realize that they'd be needed when Vincent decided what he was going to do?

As they positioned themselves, I caught a glimpse of a large black truck near the edge of the gardens and several people taking down the tents and stowing boxes and bags in the back. "Are the caterers still here?" I asked Tiny. "Shouldn't they be detained?"

"Damn!" He called to one of the men, "Johnny! Task for you." Johnny, along with the others, looked relieved that there was something to do. After Tiny told them what he needed, they headed towards the caterers' truck. So everything outside was under control; but inside, hell had come to roost.

When I gave more attention to the others in the kitchen, I noticed that Monsignor Grace was taking out his extreme unction kit. He handed the small candle to Mother Frances, who lit it as he unfolded his stole, kissed it, hung it around his neck, and made the sign of the cross before starting the prayers for the dead. As he and Mother Frances worked, Winnie bent over, reaching for the girl. Mother Frances hissed at her. "Sisters! You know your place."

"Let them be, Mother," Monsignor Grace said. "You assist me in God's work. They have another kind of work to do."

Surprise doesn't half explain what Winnie and I were feeling. Her reaction was a silent acknowledgement of his generosity and a slight wetness to her eyes. From my open mouth to my rapidly beating heart, I supposed my face was red as Santa's suit. *Do you have a trunk line to the monsignor, too, Lord? Delightful! Keep it open, please. And, thank you.*

My hands were shaking, but Winnie's were steady as she placed her fingers on the poor girl's eyes, and gently closed them. Her head tilted and her brow furrowed. It's not often I see that reaction come to Winnie. While the world surprised and perplexed me every day, she sailed through problems and celebrations with very little outward display of her feelings. "Is there something wrong?" I whispered. "Besides the dead body."

She held up the palm of her hand to me and sniffed, and

then sniffed again, motioning to me to come closer.

In order not to distract Monsignor Grace at his *Pater Nostra,* she spoke in a very low tone, asking, "Do you smell that?"

"Tea and vomit," I whispered.

"Not that. The other."

"There's another?"

She still kept her voice just above silence but her "Aggie!" was loud and clear. Winnie was not amused.

"Okay." I sniffed away from the vomit, near the girl's ear, slightly miffed but not completely surprised that Winnie had detected something I hadn't. She usually did. "Almonds? There were candy almonds on the table during dessert."

We must have looked like idiots. Two nuns half crouched in a kitchen, whispering like silly schoolgirls. But we weren't playing Gossip. This wasn't a game. At least, not to us.

"Not candy. Something just underneath the tea. Try again," she ordered.

I rolled my eyes, but did as she bade. Oh, bother it! She was right. That acrid smell that reminded me of my grandmother's penchant for lapsang souchong hit my nostrils first, but just behind it was something else, something like . . . "Smells like pits that have been left out too long after a day canning peaches."

"That's it. Not everyone can smell it. But many women can. Cyanide. Probably from rat poison."

"But where . . . ?"

She gave me a hand up and we began searching the kitchen, she in the lower cupboards, I in the upper. Nothing but mismatched plates and a complete dinner set in the upper cabinet of the Hoosier cupboard, so I started looking on all the shelves in the room. It was the first that I'd actually been able to see a kitchen where money was no object in its furnishings. This kitchen was absolutely spotless. Everything that had been used that afternoon must have been quickly washed and put away. I'd want to keep this wonderful room clean, too. If I knew how. The floors were a warm pine, with wide boards and thin ones intermixed. Such workmanship! The walls were covered with white bead board, like we had in the convent kitchen, topped with grass green molding. Lovely pale-green-and-white-striped half-curtains stretched across triple windows on one wall. All around us were pale green walls. I had been in Italians' kitchens enough to know this bright space was unusual. Someone who loved sun and God's creation had created this with great good taste and—like the front hall—joy. I could only assume it was Catherine.

She had used the hues outside the windows for her pallet. Her accessories were typical kitchen fare, but chosen for workability and beauty of design. There was a huge steel and pale yellow porcelain gas range with six burners; two ovens were built in at the side. Wouldn't my mother have loved it! No wood or coal to shovel. On one of the burners was a pristine steel teakettle, still steaming. On the opposite wall there was not one pale yellow and oak Hoosier cupboard, but two, with open steel shelves between. The shelves were topped by a slab of soapstone like the one we had at the convent. On it were canisters labeled in Italian; but it was obvious they were meant for flour and sugar, coffee and tea. The adjacent wall had storage cupboards on the bottom, with more soapstone atop. It held a huge, deep sink that was dropped into a hole in the counter. A chopping block was set nearby so vegetables could be prepared close to the sink, and overhead was a rack holding shiny copper pots.

The large central kitchen table the girl had been sitting at was covered by a pristine white cloth. Fragile, flower-strewn cups and saucers were set on it with a matching teapot. One of the cups was overturned, its dark tea staining the tablecloth. Alongside was the usual stuff that everyone needs when having tea. Milk in a cream pitcher that matched the cups and saucers.

Sugar cubes in a different bowl. Honey. A few cookies.

Wait! What was that among the sugar cubes? I tugged at Winnie's sleeve. "Whoever heard of yellowish sugar cubes?"

"They might have them in Italy, but I've never seen anything like this here. They're not uniformly yellow, but spotted. I don't like the looks of this. The poison couldn't have been in the tea, or Anna would be dead, too. So it must have been in the sugar cubes." Winnie edged over to Vincent and Richard, careful not to get in Monsignor Grace's way as he signed a cross on the girl's forehead with consecrated oil and blessed her on her way to a different world, one where these kinds of things didn't happen, where she would be safe from madmen and, possibly, poisoned sugar cubes. I scooped up the bowl with the suspect cubes.

Josiah had been quietly and reverently standing behind Mother Frances, glaring at us and what we were doing. Was it the Catholic in him, or the Cop who finally left his post and came up to give me a good pinch on my elbow. "Leave things be, Aggie," Josiah said, also in a whisper.

I noted how Vincent reared back at what Winnie was saying to him. "Not this, I can't," I said. "We need to get all the sugar cubes in this house and examine them."

Josiah grabbed my arm and tugged me into the corner. "What the hell are you doing, and why are you doing it?"

"Getting poison out of this kitchen." I waved the bowl under his nose. "Cyanide, maybe, Winnie says. Can you smell it?"

Winnie was back. "Not usually detectable until it comes in contact with saliva, Aggie. The salt in the saliva starts the reaction. The stomach acid finishes it and anyone who ingests it. Pretty much immediately."

The Cop took over. "Aren't there sugar cubes in Vincent's office?" Josiah asked.

"Yes," I answered.

"I'll get them," Richard said.

"Thanks. Vincent used some of those cubes, Winnie. And the dog had two. So did Mother Frances."

"They're not dead," Winnie said, "so they didn't eat the poisoned ones—if that's what these are."

"For crying out loud . . ."

I didn't hear the end of Josiah's rant because the door to the hall opened and Richard and a younger and slimmer version of Vincent came into the kitchen. He was a couple of inches shorter than Winnie, who was not quite as tall as a giraffe. About five-ten, I figured he was. He had sandy-colored hair and a deep dimple in his right cheek. His eyes were completely different from his brother's and nephew's. Where Dante's were a dark chocolate and Vincent's a lighter hue, Carlo's were the color they called hazel, green, flecked with gold and brown. He was trim and wiry like a boxer—his muscles were easy to detect under his lightweight summer shirt—and he was already tanned. A very handsome young man, he was probably breaking the damsels' hearts every day.

"All set," he told Vincent. "She's sleeping comfortably." He seemed more concerned about his elderly cousin than he did about the girl at the table—and not very surprised at the chaos in their kitchen. Or was he merely more resigned to tragedy? In my world a horror like this was heart-wrenching and, thankfully, almost nonexistent. In his, it might be much too frequent, so that it numbed any true humanity that might have been there in his formative years. I shuddered inwardly, realizing that wonderful Dante was born and bred to follow in his father's and uncle's footsteps.

How awful, Lord, to send a soul here to be drawn into the underworld that Dante—the real Dante Alighieri—had known so intimately and written about so eloquently.

Richard gave Winnie the sugar cubes wrapped in the napkin

and she tucked them into her pocket. Meanwhile, Monsignor Grace completed the final prayer and put away all the accoutrements of his calling. "Home for good?" he asked Carlo.

"One more year, mostly lab work and business subjects."

"How are the Jesuits treating you?"

"Just fine. Learning a lot of useless stuff, but the chem labs are great."

Winnie, as usual, had her bat ears tuned in. "Chem labs? Are you studying chemistry?"

"My major."

She looked as gleeful as a novice when they pinned on her first white cowl and veil. "You wouldn't happen to have some reagents and lab equipment here, would you?"

Vincent scowled. "Some? He's got a whole setup under lock and key in one of the sheds."

"What do you need, Sister?" Carlo asked.

"You take care of the rest here, Aggie," she said, snatching the sugar bowl out of my hands and balancing it on top of an open box of other cubes that she'd found in the cupboards. "I'll take care of this." She smiled at Carlo. "Come on. Let's go play with test tubes."

"She's in her element," I told the others.

"As are you," Monsignor Grace said.

"Neither one of them should be in their element here," Mother Frances said. "They're both nuns. Their element is at the convent, where they should be praying or doing chores."

"Perhaps some nuns are better suited for other things."

"I wonder if the new bishop would agree."

"I think he would. He was very pleased at the results when he asked for Sister Agnes' help last time. I think I will call him now and tell him what's happened. I'm going to suggest that we allow the sisters to work with the police. I'll keep them here with me and bring them back later. Meantime, why don't you prepare to leave, Mother Frances? I'm sure you're needed at the convent, and Vincent can spare someone to drive you back."

That was a dismissal, and not a gentle one. Oh, Lord, living with her for the next few days is going to be hell. Could You whisper in her ear as You whisper in mine so she doesn't take it out on the new nuns?

"My pleasure, Robert," Vincent said. "I'll get one of my men to drive her. You may use my phone in the library to call the bishop while Richard rustles up a car and driver. You shouldn't have any problem finding your way."

When Monsignor Grace left the kitchen, I thought it prudent to keep out of Mother's way. I shouldn't have bothered, because within a heartbeat she slammed out of the house and plunked down in one of the Adirondack chairs on the lawn.

"She's not too happy, is she?" Tiny asked.

"She thinks I'm sullying the sisterhood."

"And what do you think?"

"No one has ever asked me that before. I'm not sure I've even asked myself."

He smiled, and suddenly I could understand why other women would give up their independence for the opposite sex. Not me, of course. I didn't want to be saddled with a sweaty man who smelled of beer and never raised a hand to help with the house and his own children. I had never minded a flirtation or two, and had even rather liked kissing. But I never intended to be hog-tied to a brute like my Uncle Tom or a total ninny like my cousin's husband. I had always wanted an education and independence. Ironically, I'd found both in the convent— which, also ironically, tied into what Tiny had asked. "I think I'm being used by God to do something with the gifts he's given me. How can that sully the sisterhood?"

"How, indeed?" he said. "So, what now, Sister Agnes?"

Something had been niggling at the corners of my brain and

suddenly it snapped into focus. "We need photos."

"It would be my pleasure to assist you in that endeavor."

"I hoped it would."

It didn't take him long to fetch his Brownie, but forever to set up each photo. He was a perfectionist, taking angles I would never have dreamed of.

Josiah watched his every move, fuming. "What's taking him so long?"

Tiny chuckled. "He's right here beside you, trying to get the right exposure for the best contrast," he said. "Luckily, there's plenty of light in the kitchen."

"Or we'd be here till sunset, we would," Josiah said.

Tiny wound the film in the camera and covered the lens. "That should do it. Would you like to watch me print these, Sister?"

"Yes!"

"Sergeant Morgan, would you hold down the fort with Richard?" When Josiah nodded, there was much too much cunning in his averted gaze. Obviously, Tiny saw it, too. "But if you've got a notion to search the house, be warned that there are alarms and cameras in every room. Vincent may come in, guns blazing, especially after all that's happened today."

I doubted very much that there were alarms and cameras in every room. If there were, how would they record anything? But I also wanted to assure Tiny that my cousin could be trusted—or threatened. "Josiah! Give your word."

"All right, Aggie. We'll have enough to do here in the kitchen."

"If you break a promise to a nun, you will regret it for the rest of your misbegotten life. Probably much longer."

"Enough. I get it. We'll stay in the kitchen until Vincent gets back."

I followed Tiny, who had to shorten his stride several times to allow me to stay even with him. "That was something, Sister. I don't know any other woman who could have handled him so well."

"I'm not a woman. I'm a nun."

He laughed from deep inside him, a rolling laugh that was rich and melodious. "And here I thought all nuns were women."

"Not really. All nuns are girls when they enter the convent. They reach their maturity as nuns, not women."

"There's a difference?"

"Oh, yes. Most retain a childlike anticipation. Most are not afraid enough. But some are afraid too much. Afraid they will somehow fail as a nun and be damned forever to a life they don't know, or a life they fear and tried to escape for one reason or another."

"Which are you?"

"Why do you always ask me hard questions?"

"Questions that you don't want to answer?"

"Questions I've never thought about in years, or at all." When we arrived at a small shed near the tree house, he unlocked the door and snapped on the electric lights. "I thought darkrooms were supposed to be dark."

"Not at first. I have to set up the chemicals and rinsing baths. Then I'll shut off the white lights to develop the film in the dark. When I enlarge and print, I like to work with only red lights. It won't take long. Look around. Some of my photos are framed and hanging on the walls."

Some? There were dozens of delightful landscapes, cityscapes, flowers, and portraits, a handful of them delicately tinted with pink or blue or yellow. "These are wonderful! Masculine and feminine at the same time. How do you get the pastel colors?"

"Paints. The kinds that dye the paper, so the color won't fade."

"The landscapes are my favorites."

"Would you like one?"

"I'd love one, but I must decline. We aren't allowed personal adornments, not even for our walls."

"What a pity. A woman such as yourself should be surrounded by treasures she loves."

"A nun such as myself carries her treasures with her in her heart."

"I think there are not many nuns such as yourself."

"Mother Frances would say *thank God.*"

He fell silent at that, working quickly as he mixed chemicals, so I hadn't much time to finish perusing the hidey hole a grown man had made for himself. Like the gallery wall, he had lined the entire room with a kind of bark wallpaper, and the black frames of the photographs were a stark contrast on it. In one half of the room were clotheslines strung from side to side, clothespins pinned on them, some holding unframed photos. Painted shelves in several colors lined the rest of the room. Some held reams of paper, while others housed boxes and bottles of developing stuff.

"Winnie would love this place."

"You'll have to bring her some day."

"I'm fascinated by the labels. They're so graphic, like the advertisements and posters of the art deco movement in Germany."

"I got them with the Brownie 620, which is made in Germany."

He had dozens of jars with colored salts in them, and bottles with the skull and crossbones on them. Arsenic, cobalt salts, graphite . . . my heart stopped beating at the *C-Y-A* of one label. I didn't want to read the rest. I didn't have to. Had I walked into a shed with a man who might be a homicidal maniac?

Tiny came up to stand behind me, and whispered in my ear,

"Well, Sister Agnes, I guess you're one of those nuns who are not afraid enough."

CHAPTER EIGHT

If I didn't die of fright the first time I'd faced death, I wasn't going to die now. Although . . . I *was* beginning to regret giving that little gun to Richard. Not that it would have done any good. If Tiny were going to do me in, he probably wouldn't wait until I asked him to first let me load the bullets. *Lord, am I going to see you today? I'm not sure whether to be happy or sad that you're saying no.*

"I have it from the highest authority that you are not what you seem," I said, whirling to find him laughing with more gusto than he had exhibited in the kitchen. He steadied himself on the edge of the table and bent over, clutching his stomach and hiccupping at his attempts to muffle his outbursts. Drat men! Just overgrown little boys, that was what they were. And I was only a grownup girl, so, truly, Lord, I couldn't help myself. I balled up my fist and whacked him on the bicep. Unfortunately, it probably hurt me more than him.

He pretended pain, however, by rubbing the area where a flea-sized fist hit him. "You don't scare easily, do you?"

"I used to think I did. But the events of the past three months have shown me that I have a capacity to stand up to my fears, and, even better, to read people."

"And you've decided that I'm not the bogeyman?"

Bogeyman? I had had as many notorious childhood monsters as the next kid. Try as I might, however, it was hard to see Tiny in that light. At the same time, I wasn't naïve anymore. What he did for Vincent could list him in the monster category to more people than just Mother Frances, but I wasn't one of them. "Right now, you're not the bogeyman. I choose not to delve further into your activities, which are none of my business as long as they don't hurt anyone I know. I am obligated not to judge, you know."

"Or throw stones."

"Yes."

"I'm going to turn out the light now. Last chance to escape."

"I'll stay and watch, thank you."

"You're not going to be able to see anything for a while. This has to be done in pitch dark." The language he used as he explained the process was rooted in Winnie's bailiwick: developer, enlarger, emulsions, silver nitrate, baths, fixatives, exposure times. I figured later that it took about twenty minutes but seemed much less. "Done! Red light on."

In red light he moved the film from one of the baths into the wash water. "I'm going to work with the negatives wet for now and give the cops the first batch of wet prints. I'll make better prints for us later, when they have time to dry completely."

Time took on a new meaning in that dim light. I could hear my heart beat, see the shadows of things at first; but as my eyes adjusted, it felt normal for everything to have this otherworldly glow caused by the red light. Tiny's movements were lithe and precise, with no wasted motion. He chose an image to print and then put it into a big black enlarger contraption, focusing it on a piece of paper. When he was satisfied, he fiddled with the printer, waited a few moments, and then put the exposed paper into the first bath. I thought something would happen immediately. "There's no image."

"There will be. Have patience." He touched the edge of the bath, peering into it almost as intently as I was. Slowly, the paper started to change. "Now," he said.

As shapes began to float up from the developing fluid, I could hardly breathe. "Magic," I whispered.

"Yes."

Every detail of the poor girl grew from fuzzy grey to a myriad of hues of black, grey and white. Everything was sharp and as horrible as the real thing. Each crease in her dress stood out in stark relief. The grimace, the tightness of her fingers, the lifeless eyes—each gave mute evidence of a murder, and a murderer without any true human feelings.

"Let them try to dispute what happened," Tiny said.

"They ought to have a police photographer at each crime scene. Wouldn't that be an exciting career?"

"When they need them, the police borrow photographers from the *Journal.*"

"Too bad. You could apply for the job."

He snickered, but from the way he stopped for a moment and tilted his head, I knew he was thinking about it. Was he satisfied with the way things were in his life, or did his gorgeous photos show another side to him, one he had been tamping down, but would like to express more openly? In my few short years in the convent—but mostly from my last brush with murder—I had learned that life was too short to waste in idle pursuits, but too long to be chained to a heartless profession such as his.

Ah, Father, is there nothing you can do to stop this madness? Yes, I know each of us must learn to make the right choices, but when we fail to remember, could you nudge us in the right direction once in a while? Ten Commandments? Sermon on the Mount? Yes, I guess you could call them nudges. Sorry, my mistake. It's your plan, after all.

"Tell me, Tiny . . . the girl . . . who was she?"

He thought about my question as he transferred the developed print into the fixative bath. "I don't really know. Vincent hired her from an agency in Boston. She spoke with a brogue, so I assume she was from the old sod, as you Irish call it, but I don't know that for a fact."

"Did she have a name?"

"Ah, yes. Kathleen. Kathleen Killian. But she said that everyone called her Kitty."

Saints and angels! Could my lot be any more predictable? If they didn't name their girl child Mary, it was Kathleen or Maureen. Every once in a while there was a Nora thrown in for good measure. Why, if I called out Kathleen in my classroom, seven heads would pop up.

"Vincent will know the details," he said.

"Yes, I suspect he will." As he worked on the other photos, I jumped in where fools fail to go. Typical. A half hour ago I had decided it was none of my business; but I changed my mind. If I were going to have a chance of solving this for Dante, then everything about this pitiful occurrence—and the relationships surrounding it—needed to be explored. "Tell me, why do you work for Vincent?"

"I don't work for Vincent."

"But . . ."

"I'm his business partner. His father and my father came here to America together in 1888. Donato, Vincent's father, was seventeen. My father, only fifteen. And there were two other young men from our village who came with them. They pooled their small amount of money and began the import business called Montagne's."

"But that's Rhode Island's best interior design studio."

"It began as a small store that imported statues, porcelain, and home furnishings, just about anything Italian. At first, it was cheap goods, because that's all their money could buy. Gradually they learned that better merchandise meant more sales and growing profits, so they imported only the best, building an inventory and a clientele until Montagne's became what it is today."

"I thought Vincent owned a bar."

"Nope." He grinned. "We own three, along with three restaurants, a laundry service, Carlson's Jewelry Emporium, and fifty-nine tenements, the best on the Hill. Through Montagne's, we began importing hand-made tile, later branched out to tile setting, and learned about construction. So now we're thinking about investing in the Treponti Construction Company. I'm pushing the buyout because the tenements and construction parts of the enterprise are my responsibility. My cousin Matt runs the restaurants. The sons of our fathers' former partners—may they rest in peace—run the laundry service. Three of the wives oversee Montagne's and Carlson's. Vincent and his brother-in-law Mark keep the accounts and invest the money we make." He shrugged in that age-old Italian way and adopted the slang that identifies the Italians of Federal Hill, a slang he hadn't used until now. "We doing okay, eh?"

"But . . . I thought . . ."

"Thought? You mean you heard rumors and innuendo. I'm not saying there isn't some truth to it. I'm not saying there is. Ooofah! It's all business, whatever it is. Our fathers built it. We carry on the tradition."

"So that's why you've been included in the unfolding of all this, when the others were excluded. You and Vincent are equal."

"That's not how it works. He's the capo, the head of the family enterprises. The rest of us have our own business interests. But like our fathers, we pool our money, share in the profits, and put the rest away in good investments. Vincent has more responsibility because he handles all the money and oversees all the businesses. But in the long run he respects me the way I respect him."

"And it's all about respect, isn't it?"

"In a way. Our way. It works for us. Why change it?"

"Could you change it if you wanted to?"

"Could you change your family? Your honor? Your destiny?" He shook his head and turned to face me. There was hardness now, where there hadn't been before. "You don't want to know everything, Sister Agnes. And I don't want to tell you. Let's leave it at that."

He returned to the printing process, but the silence now held another burden. He hadn't said outright, but he had implied that the rumors about them were true. "I will pray for you."

"Good. And I will pray for you."

"I don't need . . ."

He dropped the wooden grips he'd been using to transfer the paper from one bath to another, whipped around and tightened his fingers around my arms. "You do. You're involved in something you've never encountered before. Maybe we all are. The way this is starting to look, it might be tied in with one guy or a whole army. It's dangerous! You have to think carefully about whether or not you want to help discover the truth. Take the word of someone who's had lots of encounters with the devil. Your last experience with a crime was a cake walk compared to this." He shook me, but it wasn't with any great force; it was more like what my father would do if he was here and afraid for me and I wasn't listening to his advice. "God damn it, woman! Catherine is dead. Kitty is dead. One was his scullery maid. But the other was Vincent's wife. His *wife!* Do you think you're immune because of your habit? There is money and power in this family, and it looks like someone is sending a message that he's out to get it. And don't forget—he got through our defenses, right here on the farm. I know Vincent said he'd do this on the up-and-up. But make no mistake, this is war."

I eased out of his grasp and took his hands in mine. "Thank you for your concern. I will consider what you said. But you have to understand that no matter what the danger is, I owe something to that little boy. Dante came to me. *Me*. You talk about honor and destiny. Well, I have my honor, too; and my gut feeling says that my destiny is linked to this, to Dante." I smiled, pushed him away, and wiped my sleeve across my eyes. "Darn my socks! There must be something in here that irritates me. Present company excluded."

He grinned. "Thanks a bunch."

He went back to work, running what looked like a long-handled rubber ruler across the finished prints, then pinning them to the ropes strung across the room. "Why did you do that?"

"Do what?"

"The rubber thing."

"Takes the liquids off the prints. Don't want spots on them distorting anything."

"Handy. Would it work on glass?"

"It should."

"We could use that in the convent and church. It takes hours to clean all those windows."

He reached under the counter and drew out three boxes with labels that said *squeegee* and a photo of the rubber thing. "My gift to the convent."

I put the three boxes in my capacious pockets. "I will give them to Mother Frances. Thank you."

We were interrupted by a knock on the door and Richard calling, "Almost finished in there? Winnie and Carlo want everyone in the front parlor."

"Two minutes," Tiny said.

It actually took five minutes before we were ready to join the others, who were once again gathered, this time in a room unlike any I'd ever seen. Afternoon sunlight streamed through several large, square windows, dappling the stone floor and huge Turkey rugs. Lush plants stood in every corner and on several tables, each vigorous and shiny with good care. There were two fireplaces, one on each end, with a grouping of furniture around each. I counted five couches and seven easy chairs, two chandeliers, several tables—one a gaming table— and more Impressionist paintings. Well, Richard had said there could be more than twenty people there at one time. This room could accommodate twice that many with room to spare.

A woman older than Anna was serving coffee and tea—this time with granulated sugar in a matching coffee service—the one I had seen in the Hoosier cupboard. She had a direct, level, intelligent, penetrating gaze. Taller than most Italian women, she still had dark hair with only a few strands of grey. Her dark eyes had a milky surface and she squinted every so often, probably trying to see through cataracts like Sister Justina's. Her features were small, delicate, hinting at the beauty she must have been.

"You like a coffee or tea, Sister?"

"Coffee, please. Cream and two teaspoons of sugar. Ella, is it?"

"*Si.* Yes."

It surprised me that unlike Anna, she knew English. But they had been here a number of years. Why wouldn't she? "I hope you're back to normal."

"*Si.* A little. More better when the *policia* get the girl outta here." She smiled all around before heading for the door. "We do a cold supper outta side. One hour."

"*Grazie,*" Vincent said, reaching down to pet Caesar, who then followed Ella out of the room. I was really glad to see the little dog was okay.

Carlo helped himself to black coffee and lounged into one of the corner chairs. "The cops are winding up their interrogation of the caterers. They said another half hour and they'll be finished."

"I'll be right back," Tiny said. "I've got to give them these prints."

"Wait one minute." I turned to Vincent. "I'd like Josiah to be here, if you don't mind."

"Whatever you wish, Sister. The police will have to know all this sometime."

An uncomfortable silence ensued until Tiny and Josiah returned. Each of us was undoubtedly lost in the same thoughts—what to do and how to do it. Finally, everyone started to talk at once, but Vincent stopped us with one word, "Silence!" Mid-sentence, everyone stopped. Such power in only two syllables. I wondered how long it took to change a Dante into a Vincent. He pointed to his brother. "You first."

"It was definitely cyanide in the sugar cubes."

Josiah whipped out his journal and pencil and began taking notes. Or doodling. I wouldn't put him past it.

Winnie added, "Probably from rat poison we found under the sink or in one of three sheds or the barn."

Carlo coughed. "Well, it could have come from my supplies. They'd have to break in, though, and the lock wasn't broken."

"Same here," Tiny said. When Vincent turned to him, eyebrows raised, Tiny shrugged. "I have a bottle to use in technique experiments."

More furious scribbling by Josiah. It was fun watching him struggle with what we were talking about. He would probably label murderer to everyone in that room, including the good monsignor, who looked a bit uncomfortable, as if he had something to say that he didn't really want to impart. Well, my goodness! He did.

"I've spoken to Bishop Keough," the monsignor said. "He's worried about the situation and wants to help the police. Since

Sister Agnes and Sister Winifred were so perceptive on the last case, he encourages you both—working with Josiah and Vincent, of course—to use your resources and to do it quickly. We're very lucky that the school year was over yesterday, because we thought you would want to start immediately. So we will excuse you from your duties for as long as it takes."

Excused from our duties? Was I prepared for the Second Coming? Funny, but I wasn't a bit scared. Probably because I didn't believe it would happen. *Wouldn't You have told me to get ready for it, Lord? What do you mean, unawares? Yes, I promise to review Revelation. As if I didn't have enough to do. Yes, I know you heard that, too. Please, no more decades until this is over. Thank you.*

"I'm not sure we need to be excused, Monsignor. Nor do I think we should be. Our best information last time came from the people in the neighborhood around St. Catherine's."

"But these murders didn't happen in your neighborhood, Sister Agnes," Monsignor Grace pointed out. "Bishop Keough, Vincent and I agree that you need to be more mobile and closer to those who could be helpful. So . . . we are prepared to give you a temporary transfer to St. Gregory's, only a few miles from here."

"My choice," Vincent said, "is to put you up in the guest house."

What? They were going to give us a vacation from Mother Frances' schedules? And here I was, about to turn it down. I should be tied to a chair and flogged with wet spaghetti.

"You are all assuming that this is the main point of attack," I said.

"You don't think so, Aggie?" Richard asked.

"No, I don't." I put down my coffee and concentrated on the thoughts that had been niggling at the edges of my consciousness all day, and that had solidified during that dark half hour in Tiny's workroom. "I think this farm is an opportunistic place, one that's more vulnerable than your own compound in the city, Vincent. As Josiah said, he and his cronies can get over that fence at any time, and so could anyone else."

"We'll fix that," Vincent promised.

"Good, but that will take time, and really doesn't matter anyway. Have there been any problems at your own houses or the businesses?" Vincent shook his head. "I think it's imperative that we stay in the city." I looked at each in turn, knowing what I was going to say next was going to be difficult for them to understand. "It's time we all faced the truth of this—that Catherine and Kitty were not the targets. You are the target, Vincent; and if they can't get to you, they might try to get *at* you—perhaps this time through Dante."

Monsignor Grace reached for the Irish Crème and poured a good draft into his coffee cup. What did he need false courage for? He'd already faced the belly of the beast—me—and was still in one piece. But skeptical. "And how, exactly, did you arrive at your conclusions?" he asked.

"It makes sense, if you consider the possibility that the sugar cubes have been in the box, poisoned, a long time. I noticed that the box was almost empty, which means it was opened before today. What if those cubes have been sitting in the kitchen for a whole year, waiting like a time bomb? It's possible, because Vincent and the family aren't here every day, so they wouldn't use up the cubes quickly. That fact works for the poisoner. He wouldn't want to be here when the bomb went off. So he could tamper with the cubes, somehow dropping diluted rat poison on them. Carlo and Winnie should be able to tell us how he did it."

"After he dropped some of the cyanide crystals in water, he'd have to let them soak to extract the poison," Carlo said.

Winnie's head was about to bob off her shoulders. She must have had a great time in the lab this afternoon. We'd have adventures to talk about that night before matins. "It wouldn't have taken long. And Ella showed me a box with medical supplies in it. I found this." She pulled out a spotless handkerchief and unwrapped it to show an ordinary eye dropper. "It's clean, but just to be sure he didn't use it, I'd suggest throwing it away."

"Or giving it to us," Josiah said, reaching for it before rewrapping it and putting it in his pocket.

"Think you can get fingerprints off it?"

"We'll try, and maybe the state coppers will try. Even though it's made of glass, it's small and round. Not going to be easy."

"But I don't understand," Monsignor Grace said. "All this transferring of the poison would have taken some time, would it not?"

"Yes, Your Eminence," I said. "So he probably didn't use that dropper. He would have gone slowly so he didn't contaminate his own domain, or kill himself inadvertently." Now I was improvising, but it began to come together. "Probably he did all this somewhere else . . . yes, that makes sense. But he would have had to know the goings-on in this house. The daily routine and Vincent's schedule, so he would know when he could gain access to the house." I turned to Vincent. "He would have wanted to do it when there was no one who could catch him, or no one who knew him. Oh, my goodness!"

"She's done it again," Winnie said. "She's got that look in her eyes. The 'why-didn't-I-see-this-before' look."

My heart gave one hard thud and stopped. Absolutely stopped. I swear! The only thing I could think to do before I went to meet my maker was to cough. Hard. So I did, and a bitter cold rushed through me before my heart clicked in again and I could draw a shuddering breath. It felt like it lasted a lifetime, but it couldn't have lasted more than a few seconds. No one had jumped up to help me.

I held up my hand, trying to collect my thoughts. Some questions had to be voiced and answered first, however—questions I truly did not want to explore. *Courage, please, Lord. That little heart jolt thing? Am I laughing? Not funny. Pretty scary, in fact. Could you keep them down to a minimum?*

"Richard," I asked, "was Catherine supposed to be on the farm the day she was murdered?"

"I have no idea."

"Does anyone know if she was scheduled to be here?"

"Not me," Tiny said.

Vincent and Carlo merely shook their heads.

"Then how did she get here?"

CHAPTER NINE

More than one of the group reached for that Irish Crème. I held out my cup to Winnie, who poured a good dollop into it. False courage or not, the warmth worked as I and the others faced the truth. Besides, as all Irish know—liquor is good for the heart. Just ask my Uncle Tom, who always kept his heart nice and healthy by sleeping it off under the table.

"What you're saying—it isn't possible."

"Where have I heard that before?" I tried to get my thoughts in order, but the only thing that got through was rather simple. "I think someone she knew brought her here."

"And then . . . ?" Winnie was having trouble voicing it, but she wasn't the only one.

"And then murdered her. It must have gone that way. She saw something or heard something she shouldn't have. Maybe she caught him exchanging the sugar cubes. Maybe she heard him talking on the phone, laying down plans for Vincent's upcoming death. Maybe she got hysterical or tried to run away, maybe she threatened him with telling Vincent. Maybe she didn't even know what she heard or saw, but the murderer couldn't take a chance that she did. I said this was an opportunistic place. I didn't know how right I was."

Carlo buried his face in his hands. "Someone she knew killed Catherine? Dante's mother. Vincent's wife."

He raised his head and the youth had been replaced by a man whose visage had hardened in front of our eyes. Did everyone in Vincent's family always have quick hatred floating beneath a smooth façade? One more reason that Winnie and I had to find this killer before any of them did—before it began to pollute Dante at too young an age. But what age was okay to hate that much? And when did it start?

I sighed at the futility of it all. "I think that's the way it happened, yes. She could have taken a cab, I suppose; but what cab would come all the way here?"

"Any cabbie who wanted to earn a monthly wage in one day," Richard said.

"But wouldn't she have wanted him to wait to take her back?"

Grudgingly, he said, "Seems likely."

"So why didn't he notify Vincent when she didn't come out to the cab?" It was so frustrating! No one ever wanted to believe that ordinary people did terrible things. But they did. "Nothing fits unless we consider that she knew her killer. She could have hired a cabbie, but then he would have been sent away by someone else—the killer, of course. But after the accident report hit the front page of the *Journal,* the cabbie would have read about the death on the farm. Wouldn't he wonder what had happened and why he had been sent away? Wouldn't he want to tell someone what had happened? That would put him in danger from the killer, who would have to eliminate him, too. That's terribly complicated, when it was probably much simpler. She came with someone she knew, and he killed her."

"*Why?*"

"I don't know yet."

"Jesus," Vincent said, and began pacing again, the way he'd been doing in the library a couple of hours earlier. "I don't know what the hell is happening. Someone she knew. God damn it to hell! That means he's probably been under my nose the past year—probably part of our organization. Was he quietly planning to kill again? Was he laughing at what he'd done? Was he watching every day to see if his plan had finally worked?" He threw his cup across the room and it shattered against the corner of the fireplace. Quickly, he strode over to the door and locked it. "I don't want Ella or Anna more upset. If they see me like this, it will scare the wits out of them."

He plopped into a chair next to Monsignor Grace, who grasped his shoulder and gave it a squeeze. "We should listen to Sister Agnes, Vincent. She may have more information."

"It's not information," I said. "It's just deduction."

"Whatever it is," Vincent said, "it sounds right. I don't want to believe it, but it sounds right. So go on. If there's more, I can take it."

"All right. So we'll assume she did come with someone she knew. When he killed her, it was really violent. That blow to her forehead, for example. Several things could have caused that kind of horrific reaction. Fear. True madness. Revenge. Envy. Greed. Takes in a lot of the seven deadly sins."

"I wonder which one we're dealing with," Monsignor Grace ruminated.

"We will soon find out, never fear."

Richard looked as if he would jump out of his skin. "Why put Catherine in the car?"

"I'm not sure. But of this I am sure: no matter why he killed, unless he were a true madman he'd be flushed with fear of being caught. Nobody wants to get caught. When an ordinary person commits a crime, doesn't he want to get away with it?"

Vincent's jaw was so tight it was a wonder his teeth didn't snap in two. "What," he said, "makes you so sure that this was an ordinary person?"

"I'm not sure. I'm not sure about anything. But I read the papers and hear the news from my students. And I've seen *Public Enemy*. Professional killers either have a way out so they don't get caught, or they don't need one because no one will talk, no matter what. Beg your pardon, but you all ought to know that. Besides," I stared him down, "this was no ordinary *victim*. This was your wife. You would turn over rocks to find her killer—the way you want to right now."

"I've given my word that I will help find this killer, but not cause any problems—for the police or the Diocese."

Score one for Monsignor Grace! "All right then . . . we have a murderer who doesn't want to get caught. The first thing he'd need to figure out was how to deal with the body. Leaving her where he killed her or dumping her somewhere probably occurred to him. But that wouldn't help. Any and all of you were bound to miss her right away. And remember that Catherine wasn't his intended target. I think she just got in his way and he didn't want attention to focus on his real crime—killing Vincent and getting away with it. So he had to come up with the accident scene. The fake accident scene that put the police off the hunt for a murderer and gave him plenty of time to get away from the trap he'd dug himself into when he killed Catherine. He needed more time, enough time to see if his poison would work, or if he had to get to Vincent another way."

"Damn! I feel like such an idiot," Carlo said. "I argued with Vincent when he cursed the cops for not investigating Catherine's death." He turned to his brother. "You were right all along, and all I wanted to do was to get things back to normal. I'm surprised you don't hate me for that."

"Why? Getting back to normal was important. Dante needed that."

"Wait a minute. Wait a minute. Wait a minute," Josiah said, "I missed something here, cousin. I can follow your line of reasoning, and I'm going to tell the captain that it's probably the way it happened."

"Probably?"

"Aggie, it sounds good, but there's something else wrong here."

"And that is?"

"Why the sugar cubes?"

"Josiah! Why, you're turning into a good detective. I take back everything bad I said about you when we were kids." I was joking with him, but he had brought up a good point. Why, indeed, the sugar cubes? "Vincent, besides you and Caesar, who in this house eats sugar cubes?"

"I don't know."

"No one does," Carlo said. "We all use regular sugar."

"And I only use a couple each afternoon," Vincent said, "when I have my daily citrus drink, an old Italian remedy for dyspepsia problems."

"Does it work?" Josiah asked.

I glared at him, then remembered his two bouts with childhood cramps that the doctors finally diagnosed as dyspeptic ulcers.

"Haven't had any problems since I began drinking it."

"Which brings us back to the sugar cubes," Carlo said, "and the big question. Who did this?"

This time I didn't admonish him. Unfortunately, if my calculations were correct, he would have enough to worry about soon—in about three minutes.

"Don't ask those kinds of questions," Winnie warned, "or we'll have another Plato lesson."

"You mean the lesson about not being able to see what's in front of our noses?"

"Too late," Winnie muttered.

I wasn't trying to be prideful or arrogant. Truly I wasn't, Lord. All right, maybe a little. It did feel good to listen to the others' anger and observe their frustration, and then arrive at a conclusion that answered all the questions. Don't be smug? Oh! All right, I shall modulate my tone. I do tend to teach all the time.

"I'm sorry if this sounds pompous; but it's true," I said. "We see what a person wants us to see, not what we must see. Vigilance and attention to detail. They're what are important. Not enough of us do that." *And for that, Lord, I will say another decade of the sorrowful mysteries. You want* two? Darn my socks! I was going to be on my knees until doomsday. "For example, am I correct in assuming that Anna isn't the one who usually serves your afternoon drinks?"

"How could you know that?" Vincent asked, swiveling his head to the side and glaring at the occupant of the sofa. "Unless you asked Tiny."

"Nope, she didn't ask me."

"Anna speaks no English," I said. "But Ella does because she learned it from serving the family and your friends and associates. Oh, it's not perfect English. No elderly woman—or man, for that matter—who's spoken a foreign language all her life would be able to speak perfectly. She tries, though; and I commend her for it." I drained my cup and rose to refill it. "And she does make wonderful coffee. Is that a hint of orange in it, I wonder?"

"You'll have to ask her yourself," Vincent said. "Is that all, Sister?"

"No. That's the reason sugar cubes were served to us and the reason Mother Frances used some—because it was Anna who made up the drinks tray and not Ella."

"You think Anna did this, Aggie?"

"No, Josiah. Well, I don't really know for sure. Although at her age, I don't suppose she has the strength to bash in someone's skull. I just know that little things coincided today. Winnie was here by invitation from Vincent. Her being here meant that Catherine's murder finally came out. Ella was napping when we were parched, so Anna prepared the drinks things, adding the bowl with the sugar cubes, which would not normally be on the drinks tray, but would be in the kitchen—I noticed you usually get your sugar on a napkin."

"That's true."

"So Anna made a mistake. But please don't tell her or she'll blame herself for the maid's death."

"Don't worry, I won't."

"To continue with the coincidences, we have tea being served in the kitchen with a complete china service, with one exception—a sugar bowl that didn't match the set." I turned to Winnie and Carlo. "Were there poisoned cubes in the bowl in the office?" They both shook their heads. "So the poisoned cubes were only in the mismatched bowl."

"It wasn't really a mismatched sugar bowl," Vincent said. "It belongs to the set we . . ."

". . . use for the family?"

"Yes."

"I thought so. But only *you* use sugar cubes, so if you were going to have coffee or your citrus drink, would you take the cubes out of the family sugar bowl?"

"Certainly. Why not?"

"Ergo, having the poisoned sugar in the family sugar bowl inadvertently led to the maid's death. Until she died, we couldn't connect Catherine's death to a real attempt on Vincent. Now we can." I had to stretch my hands, which had tightened as the truth began to unfold. "Good luck for us today. Bad luck for the murderer and Kathleen Killian." I shook my head. "Kathleen Killian. Now that's another part of this puzzle that no one saw."

Everyone seemed surprised, but only my dear cousin jumped in and showed how obtuse some men were. "Who's Kathleen Killian?" Josiah asked.

"Oh, for crying out curds, cousin! You've been dealing with

her body in the kitchen. The maid. Kathleen Killian is what she called herself. I don't know what her real name is, but she certainly isn't Kathleen Killian. I believe you will discover that she ran away from home so she couldn't be questioned by the police about a murder. Probably running from the IRA, too. I hear their courts mete out immediate but not always just justice."

"Whoa! Back up, Aggie! What murder?" Josiah stopped making notes and looked so skeptical that I wanted to hit him.

"I'm getting to that. I need to start at the beginning, when we first saw her body."

"Let her do it her way," Winnie said. "It will be faster."

I knew that wasn't a real compliment, but I was feeling charitable at the moment, so I smiled anyway. "Let's start with what was out of place in that kitchen—besides the sugar bowl. First, I noticed that her cross was fastened to a chain that was long enough to be hidden inside her dress. She didn't want it to be seen by anyone, you see. But when she clutched at the neckline of her frock during the initial stage of poisoning, she pulled it out. I've seen other crosses like that. There was a display of them in Carlson's window just before St. Patrick's Day. The chain and the curlycues around the pearls are the best Florentine gold, if I remember the sign correctly, although the cross was hand wrought in County Cork. Ask the wives about it if you don't believe me. They will know. I'm convinced Kitty invented her name, probably knowing how nostalgic most Irish are about Killarney. I mean, really, what Irish mother would saddle her daughter with Kathleen Killian? The girl would have been teased unmercifully. You know . . . Kuh, Kuh, Kuh, Katie."

Monsignor Grace coughed, and he and Vincent exchanged amused glances. Good. I was afraid they were both irritated at my suppositions. "I believe you will find that she was involved in that riot in Belfast about a year ago where two Catholic girls were killed by a group of Belfast thugs—two of them girls themselves. How clever she was to insert herself into an Italian household, but not just any Italian household. Vincent's. Who would think to look for her here? And Vincent's, um, occupation would afford her creature comforts of a sort, and safety. She was dead wrong about that, of course."

I let that sink in before I went on with what I thought had been done. "Oh, yes—and before you ask—I deduced that she was Protestant because she wears a cross but no medals. A Catholic girl of her age would never be on her own without the protection a medal can give her unless she was a . . . well, a working girl of the kind that is other than a scullery maid. But this Kitty was too refined for that—and really too refined for working here. Her jewelry was too expensive. Her fingernails were manicured, not blunt cut like most servants."

"And all nuns," Winnie said.

Oh, good. She was beginning to understand the complications that were developing in *this* mystery. If we were lucky, we'd be able to solve this quickly and set this family back to order—for Dante's sake. But I was beginning to think it would take divine intervention.

"You're right, Winnie. You *can* compare our nails to hers. Hers should have been worse *if* she had been a maid in Ireland. They aren't. She must have taken good care of them here the way she had done at home. Add that observation with my other suspicions and I believe we'll find that her family is rich and Protestant, and they sent her here to hide her away. You might want to check her references, Josiah. The agency she came from should have her history on file. The most glowing reference will, of course, come from her family. It's so ironic. If the murderer wasn't so intent on getting to Vincent, Kitty might have gotten away with her own murderous act."

"You really think Kitty was a murderer?" Carlo asked. "But

that's preposterous. She was a servant. She couldn't have planned a murder. She did nothing unless we or Ella asked her to. And then sometimes Ella had to show her how."

"Which only confirms my suppositions. Remember, Josiah, Aunt Flossie was a maid to some of Newport's finest. Oh, not the ones on the Avenue, but her employers were rich enough. She always told me that a good maid was trained by housekeepers or previous employers to respond to problems as they arose or to anticipate problems before they arose. Therein lies the worth of a good servant, she always said. That Kitty waited for you to tell her what to do is more of a sign that I'm correct. Of course, Josiah will have to confirm all of this."

"But you don't need to be convinced by the police, do you, Sister Agnes?" Monsignor Grace said. "Nor do I. It's very plausible as you tell it."

I could be very persuasive, even to myself—but only if I were certain that I was right. Other times I shake in my brogans and can't keep odds and ends together. The monsignor was an astute listener, and he had a good mind. If he thought my conclusions were plausible, I could stop shaking now.

But Carlo was another story. His disbelieving sneer caught the monsignor's attention, and he leaned over to touch his arm. "You must have liked her a lot, son."

Carlo seemed confused and angry, but he was holding it all together. "Yes, I did."

Perhaps he pictured Kitty as a girl for himself. It would never have worked, of course, but men are always suckers for waifs, even those only posing as waifs.

"So, let me get this straight," Josiah said. "This maid murdered some girl in Ireland and came here to hide."

"Yes. I remember reading about it in the *Journal*. They only found one of the girls, and she was in France, posing as an au pair. Why not the other girl coming here to do pretty much the same thing until it all blows over?"

Josiah was still scribbling in that notebook. "Is she *our* murderer?"

"I don't know for sure, but I hardly think it likely. She murdered during a riot at a college. She didn't plan it. It just happened. I think it's only coincidence that she was here, in the wrong place at the wrong time, so she died by the hands of Catherine's murderer. If she hadn't, we wouldn't know that Catherine's murder is really tied to an attempt on Vincent."

"So there's also a loony out there who wants to kill Vincent."

"Yes, I think there is," I said.

"Why?"

"If we find the who, we'll find the why."

"Why don't we get some supper," Vincent said. "Let's drop this for now and regroup after we eat."

"I think that's a good idea," Monsignor Grace said. He got up and offered his arm to me. "May I escort St. Catherine's resident detective?"

Resident demon, more like it—at least according to Mother Frances. I wondered what chores she'd pile on after this day's disappointment. Or how many times she'd tell me I was a bad nun. She didn't need to remind me. I worried about that every day.

Josiah excused himself to go back to Providence with his men, and he promised to look into Kitty's credentials and family. "Your Ella packed us a cold supper to eat on our way back, Vincent," he explained. "I'll contact you in the morning if there's anything new. But most of this can be handled by the locals and the state cops. *We'll* be looking out for you, though, the whole lot of you. If anything happens on the streets of Providence, we'll be Johnny-on-the-spot. You have my word for that."

After he left, Carlo slammed his fist into the doorjamb.

"Damn! Now they have an official reason to stick their noses into our business. We have to—" He stopped short when Vincent shook his head and swiveled his gaze to Winnie and me. "Sorry, Sister Agnes. I know he's your cousin, but we've had a miserable time with the coppers."

"I know. That goes along with the territory, though, doesn't it?"

"That'll teach you not to underestimate this particular woman," Richard teased.

Everyone was silent when we stepped onto the terrace where a cold supper was laid. I looked around for Dante.

"I sent him home with Rachel and Mark," Vincent said. "He'll be staying with them for a few days. Excuse me, please. I have to see to the rest of my men, who are having sandwiches in the game room." He hung back to talk to Tiny, who nodded at what he said. All I could catch of the conversation were two words: *first watch*. Darn my socks! Men had all the fun and excitement—playing lookout had been one of my favorite childhood games. While they were hard at it, I would be peeling potatoes until Christmas.

I loaded my plate with two different kinds of salad—one of them my favorite mozzarella and tomato concoction and the other a complicated antipasto, complete with those yummy salty anchovies. There was cold, sliced roast chicken, sandwich fixings with crusty bread, a fruit bowl, and—good heavens!—a hog's head in the middle of the table. Richard caught me staring at it and had to turn away to laugh. Tiny, however, sliced off a piece for himself and put it on his plate, heaping some mushrooms over it. He offered me one and I bit into a delicious briny flavor. "Ella makes it from wild mushrooms she picks here on the farm."

"Delicious. Is that *thing* there any good," I asked him.

"Do you like pork?"

"Love it. But I've never eaten something with ears and a nose before." I loved his laugh; it was so honest and exuberant.

When he could talk again, he said, "Sure you have. It's called bologna." He sliced off a small piece and dropped it on my plate. "Try some. It's the sweetest part of the hog. I guarantee you'll come back for more."

He was right. I went back twice, but averted my eyes as I sliced into the poor staring thing. They probably named this one Reginald.

The meal was over much too soon and after we all refreshed ourselves, we once again gathered in that spacious front room for a final cup of Ella's delicious coffee. The day had gone and the farm's isolation was palpable. I felt the urge to whisper, and apparently everyone did, too, because they took seats closer together than they had been before supper.

Monsignor Grace poured a small glass of anisette for himself and sipped it as everyone else settled. He looked so imposing, standing there against the mantel. His always unruly hair was more unruly than ever, but that was the only thing out of place. The rest looked as if he had been dressed by a discerning butler. He was sporting an intricate cross hanging over his cassock—gold and silver with imbedded pieces of jade, or was it Connemara marble? He wasn't Irish—at least not all Irish—because he had that refined manner that bespoke French or other European lineage. He was handsome, I gave him that much. Clear brown eyes and a slight shadow of a beard were positively attractive to any woman with a heartbeat. Of course, I was a nun, not a woman. Ha!

Presently, he put down his glass and walked over to the window where the setting sun's red glow streamed into the room. "I wonder if this is the time," he said.

Winnie raised her eyebrows at me and all I could do was shrug. Was the liquor getting to him?

It was impatient Carlo who asked what we were all thinking. "The time for what?"

"The time to figure out the real reason for this murder."

CHAPTER TEN

He came back and leaned his elbow on the mantel. "All afternoon something has been bothering me, something I don't want to think about, but must. Vincent, you don't have to answer this; but it would help if we all knew the answer to one question. Is there anyone . . . anyone at all . . . who is out to wrest power from you? To take over the Providence territory, thinking they can while your father is so gravely ill?"

Well, finally someone had said it—what I had been thinking, fearing. Silence stretched on as Vincent concentrated on turning his cup around and around on the saucer, sloshing some of the coffee over the rim. Perhaps he was thinking about answering, or trying to formulate an answer, or calculating how to shut us all up permanently without drawing attention to himself. Oh, good grief! I'd seen *Public Enemy* once, and that was once too often.

If anyone saw Vincent on the street, James Cagney was the last person they'd think of. Vincent was only a skosh shorter than his brother and handsome, with a strong body kept tightly under control. He was at times affable, loving to his son, and smart. He was also quiet, commanding, and more secretive than the Vatican. But he was being backed into a corner by a very high representative of the Church and the circumstances of his wife's death. It must have been unfamiliar territory. But, then, everything about this day and his wife's death was unfamiliar territory.

In a James Cagney moving picture, I'd expect a growl from the gangster, but not from Vincent, the lion in his den. One came anyway. He set his cup aside and levered himself out of his chair, beginning to pace in a tight circle in front of us. After three revolutions he stood at the window, staring out as the sun set and the day ended.

"There was always a chance that someone stupid would make that play. Until today I never suspected that it was possible to penetrate my organization. I am not a familiar figure to most Rhode Islanders. My name doesn't appear on any letterheads. You'll never see my signature on any bank or legal documents. My father, Donato Alberto Ricci, is *capo in ufficio*—the official boss—and will be until he dies. Then the title passes to me. For all intents and purposes, I am invisible, only an eldest son. Yet I and my partners control far more than anyone knows, including the police."

"And do you trust your partners?" Monsignor Grace asked.

"With my life. We are bound by honor and family. Whoever is doing this has no honor, no family, and if we ever get our hands on him, no life."

"But you don't know who it is?"

"No."

"No guesses?"

"We don't operate that way. Guessing works sometimes, for little things. Guessing who's thieving here and there from our revenues or who's bribing people in embarrassing positions, these things we can do. But my father taught me that guessing usually brings big problems. If you're wrong, more deaths, and an instability that could crush us faster than these maggots can pick away at our flesh."

He turned around and came to stand in front of me. "Sister, I don't often ask for help."

"He never asks for help," Tiny said. "He's never needed any, because he's always smarter than the other guy."

"This time I'm dealing with the death of my wife and I don't feel so smart, so I'm asking for your help. This afternoon I expected it, even demanded it. But on more reflection, I can't do that to you. It's too dangerous. So, if you refuse, I will understand and will not hold it against you."

"I will be glad to help you . . . on one condition."

"Ah," he said, a sad smile changing the intensity of his chiseled features, "blackmail. That I understand."

"No blackmail. If you refuse, I will understand and will not hold it against you."

Tiny smiled broadly. "She gave you back your own words, Vincent. I think she's learning how to play this game."

"Let's hear it, Sister," Carlo said.

"For his protection, I'd like Dante to be housed with the Franciscan Brothers at their school and center in Newport, starting as soon as he gets back from his aunt's. Tomorrow, if possible. And I don't want anyone but those in this room to know where he is. Not one person. You must know why, Vincent."

I thought he was going to pace again; instead, he put his hand on my shoulder. A hand that shook with the emotion he did not show.

"I was thinking of sending him to Italy."

"That would alert your men, who might talk to the wrong person. We don't know who this monster is, so we all have to be discreet. But now that I think about it, you *could* tell people that he's going to Italy. Under the circumstances, everyone who knows about this murder on the farm would expect it. It would be good cover, because we'd throw your enemy off the tracks by keeping Dante here where we can get to him quickly if need be. I'm sure Monsignor Grace can arrange it so that his residence at the Franciscan Center would be as secret as entering a monastery."

"Absolutely," Monsignor Grace said. "Will Richard be accompanying him?"

"I guess I should have asked for two conditions."

"And the other is . . . ?" Vincent asked.

"That you let me arrange protection for him."

"You have better protection than me?"

"No one's better than you, Richard, but this time you would be a liability. On the other hand, my friend, Mrs. Stanford Vandergelder has protection that's just as good. She will do what I ask and will ask no questions. Her home . . ."

"Mansion," Winnie said. "Twenty-four rooms, seven bathrooms, a ballroom, a score of servants, and an indoor pool."

"Her *home* is protected twenty-four hours a day with highly paid security people. She has dozens of bodyguards round the clock—bodyguards who are not well known here in Rhode Island. And she lives on Bellevue Avenue, only two miles from the Franciscan Center, so there will be extra trained men available if anything out of the ordinary happens." I laid my hand atop Vincent's. "Let's face it—if Richard leaves when Dante does, then everyone will speculate that they're together. Your enemy only has to find Richard and he'll have Dante. This way we can hide him among young boys his own age, and he can have a great summer vacation, different but safe because Mrs. Vandergelder's men can be on the grounds, dressed as Franciscans, by Dante's side every minute. Meanwhile all of us can put our heads together to find out the truth."

"How does she know this Vandergelder woman?" Tiny asked Richard.

"Aggie saved her from drowning. Jumped into the surf below the Cliff Walk to pull her out. Nearly drowned herself when her skirts got wet and tangled around her legs."

"*Dio mio!*"

"That's my . . . our Aggie."

Am I blushing, Lord? Well, stop it, can't You? What am I saying? That's what being unmasked does to me.

"That's Sister Agnes to you, Richard."

"You'll always be Aggie to me."

"Hair butcher."

"Eternal pest."

Twenty years melted away as we grinned like the children we had been together. Where had the years gone? He had been my friend then; he was my friend now. I gloried in knowing that no matter what paths we had chosen or would choose, our friendship would never change. Although I was really glad he couldn't get the glue pot out again. He'd be disappointed at the clumps of shorn locks that lay matted under my veil from the constriction of my caplet. Nothing to glue, nothing to give pleasure to onlooker or self—such is the life of a Merciful Sister of Mary.

"Do we have a deal?" I asked Vincent.

"Deal. How will we get Dante to Newport?"

"I shall call Mrs. Vandergelder at the crack of dawn tomorrow morning. She will send her chauffeur and a bodyguard. You should not go with him, Vincent."

"None of us will. It's up to you, now, Sister. You and one of Newport's four hundred and the Church."

A half hour later I leaned back and shut my eyes as Vincent's driver took us back to the convent in Vincent's wonderfully comfortable Lincoln brougham. I had protested that any old car would do, but he had insisted, and I was really grateful, now, that I let him win the argument. First stop, the monsignor's quarters, then on to the convent.

"Do you think he really meant it," Winnie whispered as we rode through the dark country roads towards the city.

We were riding in the back seat together, the three of us, with our heads within a few inches of each other because we didn't want the driver to hear about the meeting and all the decisions we had made. To make absolutely sure we weren't the ones to give away our plans, I also whispered, "That he would leave it up to us, with no interference from him?"

"Yes."

"Not in the least. I suspect they are making their own plans, expecting the worst and getting ready for it."

"He says he doesn't have any enemies who would do this," Winnie pointed out.

"Balderdash. He chose his words carefully. It's probably true that he doesn't know precisely who is at fault, but I'd bet dollars to donuts that he has some idea which of his enemies want to take over this state."

"Why wouldn't he tell us?" Monsignor Grace asked. "I've worked with Vincent before. He's always been secretive but fair. He knows we have his and Dante's welfare at heart. I prefer to think he told us as much as he knows."

"Let's pray that he did," I said, taking up my rosary. "The sorrowful mysteries, Winnie?"

"That seems best."

"I will lead," Monsignor Grace offered. "In the name of the Father and of the Son and of the Holy Ghost . . ."

The rosary always calmed me. I needed calming after this day. I needed not to think, just to pray. Damson plums! I couldn't even keep my mind on the initial prayers. They were past *The Lord's Prayer* and the three *Hail Marys* and onto the *Glory Be* and I joined in as Monsignor Grace began the first sorrowful mystery. The agony in the garden. What an amazing mystery. To me, Christianity was based on it, not really the cross. I could picture Him kneeling there in the garden of Gethsemane, taking on all our sins, bleeding from every pore. I closed my eyes and entered the spirit of the prayers.

"Hail Mary, full of grace . . ."

"We're on the second part," Winnie said.

Blast! "Holy Mary, Mother of God . . ."

I wondered what it was like to be His mother, to have to watch Him die on the cross. His agony in the garden, hers at the foot of a cross. How horrible did it have to be for a mother's heart to break? Or how good did she have to be to have such faith in her own son? Darn my socks! There I went again. Why couldn't I concentrate? Where were they now? *Glory be . . .* okay, I could slide in here. I opened my mouth to join Winnie and Monsignor Grace when a loud retort shattered the quiet. The driver swerved and speeded up.

"We've got company," he cried. Another retort echoed eerily. "Shots. Brace yourselves. I'll have to outrun them." The car swerved and teetered, then righted itself just before another shot rang out.

". . . As it was in the beginning is now and ever shall be, world without end . . ."

Winnie had the right idea. *You listening, Lord? Got some ideas? Trust in the driver? It's so hard, when I should be doing something to help!*

I scooted up on the seat and leaned over.

"You shouldn't do that, Sister."

"You can't shoot and drive at the same time, can you?"

"You want me to shoot?"

"*They're* shooting!"

"Okay. Can you hop into the front?"

It only took a moment to hoist one of my legs up and to slip over the back. I got caught on the upholstery and ended up with my veil hooked onto the shift and my leg stuck on the door handle.

"Need some help?"

"Nope." I struggled to pull my leg off the handle, control my veil, and tame my skirts. By the time I had everything under reasonable control, I was breathing fast. I heaved myself next to him. "What can I do?"

"Grab the wheel and keep the car on the road." When I tried to reach the outside of the steering wheel, he took both my hands and put them on the right. "Just keep her steady."

"Sure. I can do that."

Where was the road? Ah, the headlamps. The light they threw forward barely reached the edges of the road. My grip was steady but the road was bumpy and winding like a bloody snake. *Sorry, Lord.*

"Aggie, get back here!"

"Can't now, Winnie. Busy. You two should probably get off the seat and onto the floor."

I couldn't see them, because I had to concentrate on not landing us in a ditch, but I could hear them plop down into the well of the back seat.

The driver stuck his head out of the window and pulled a really big gun from inside his jacket. I caught a glimpse of a leather grip and some straps. He hung out the window, shooting back at the car behind us, and I steadied our car so it wouldn't rock and fall off into nothing. Several shots rang out at once, and I couldn't tell what had come from the idiots behind us and what had come from us. A bullet must have hit something underneath the car because the noise was different, a dull, hollow, cracking sound. At the same time, the driver's gun flew up in the air and landed in my lap. I looked over at him. He was grimacing and sweat stood out on his forehead. And then I saw the blood. It was oozing out of a gaping wound on his gun hand.

"Winnie, your handkerchief."

"You've got one of your own."

"There's chalk and squeegees and tons of other stuff in my pocket. Just hand yours over."

"What for?" She stuck her head above the seat and caught a glimpse of the driver's wound. "Lord, have mercy!" She waved the handkerchief in my face and I lifted one hand to bat it out of the way.

"I can't see." Suddenly I realized this wouldn't work. "I can't take my hands off the wheel, so you're going to have to tie up his hand."

"*Me?*"

"Yes!" I knew she had an aversion to blood. "If you don't do it, we might have more sticky red stuff than this. On you."

She gasped but quickly shook out her handkerchief and tied it tightly around the man's hand, then collapsed back into the well beside Monsignor Grace, who was still praying the rosary. I gave my attention for a split second to the man beside me. Uh-oh! The driver and I looked at each other and we realized that the handkerchief was going to make it impossible for him to close his grip around the gun and insert his finger in the trigger.

Oh, how I wished I hadn't given Richard my nice little gun. There was nothing else for it. The big one would have to do.

CHAPTER ELEVEN

I looked over to the beefy man cradling his bandaged hand, holding it carefully. Damson plums! Out of commission. Blast! Blast! Blast! One of us had to be able to fend off the hounds of hell on our tail. Winnie was cowering on the floor in the back. Monsignor Grace was praying up a storm, but not making any move to do anything else. So guess who was elected?

"Can you drive?" I asked the wounded man.

"Sure."

"Good. Take over." He grasped the steering wheel with his good hand. I leaned over the back of the seat and poked Winnie.

"What, Aggie?"

"Hold this."

She took one look and squealed.

"Just for one minute."

She held the gun gingerly between her thumb and middle finger. "Please hurry."

"Are there other bullets?" I asked the bleeding man next to me.

"In the glove box."

The glove box held a flashlight and a small arsenal of ammunition. "Are these for the same gun?"

"Yep."

I scooped up one of the boxes and tossed it onto the back seat, where it landed softly. I followed right after, my knees smacking into a hard shoulder or two. Or maybe a head. Once again my full skirts got in the way. Why did we wear these clumsy things? Is there any real advantage? Well, it probably wasn't every nun who found herself in these kinds of situations and needed more mobility than the skirt afforded. I gave one final heave, and my brogan struck what felt like a shoulder but might have been an eye.

"Ooof! Aggie, have mercy."

"What are you doing, Sister Agnes?"

"Don't worry, Your Eminence. Keep praying. I know what I'm doing, but I sure could use help from above."

Regardless of what I'd told Monsignor Grace, I only hoped I knew what I was doing. No, I did know. Maybe. It was simple. Maybe. Put bullets into the gun so there was a full cylinder. Open the back windshield. Shoot. Simple. Working on a wing and a prayer, I stuffed five bullets into the empty holes of the cylinder, then held out the ammunition box.

"Give me the gun, Winnie, and hold this."

"Oh, not again, Aggie."

"It's only a box this time."

"Oh."

After she took the box, I pulled on the latch that kept the back windshield closed. Blast and blast! It was stuck and I had to bang on it with the butt of the gun.

"I wouldn't do that, Sister!" the driver yelled. "It might go off!"

"Aggie!"

Guess I *didn't* know what I was doing. I put the gun down on the top of the seat and pulled on the handle *hard*. The latch gave, so I was able to push the window all the way open. Now what? I took a quick peek. The car was only a few feet behind us, coming up fast, faster than we were traveling; and I fully expected them to crash into us any minute or speed up to the side, where they could pick off the driver. If they did that, we were dead for sure.

"Can you go faster?" I yelled above the air *whoosh*ing in, the screech of tires and the *bang, bang, bang* of bullets.

"Not safely!"

"Are you kidding? What's safe about getting killed?!"

We picked up a little speed, but the swaying of the car increased, and since he was swerving from side to side to make us an elusive target, more speed was probably as dangerous as the bullets. It was all up to me. Good thing my father had taught me how to shoot early and often. I'd never forgotten, and, really, I did love the feel of a gun in my hands.

Never one this size, however. The barrel was long and the grip was bigger than any I'd ever held. But I didn't have a choice. I had to get them right between the eyes.

No, not literally, Lord. Goodness, how could You think that of me?

Human eyes, out of bounds. But the eyes of the car would do.

I slipped up onto the seat, kneeling off to the side so the people in the other car couldn't see the white of my cowl. Bracing my right forearm on the back of the seat, I sighted down that long barrel and lined up my first shot. It had to work, because one shot would alert them and they'd shift their attention to me and the open windshield.

Lord, shift your attention from that stupid, ugly man in Germany and give me a tiny thought, please.

"Our Father, who art in heaven . . ."

"Oh, God, she's praying. We're going to die."

"Not if I can help it, Winnie." My finger tightened, squeezing, squeezing. "Dad blast it! It's stuck!"

"Not stuck, Sister. Sight a little low and then squeeze hard!"

"Why low?"

"There's going to be a kick."

The first time I shot—when my father had taught me—the kick nearly landed me on my bottom, so I knew what he was warning. Lining up the shot below the light, I used two hands, pulling as hard as I could. The shot threw me back a bit, but I caught myself in time to hear the unmistakable shattering of glass. One of the headlamps behind us went black.

"Yahoo! You did it, Sister!"

"Not quite!" Quickly, I lined up another shot and *blam!* The second headlamp bit the dust of the road. "They're driving blind! Go! Go!"

The driver went as fast as he could, but it was soon apparent that we weren't being followed, so he worked the shift to a grinding sound, and then we slowed way down. We came into the town of Scituate, coasted through the dimly lit streets, and pulled into the parking lot next to the town hall. The car bucked a couple of times and then skidded to a stop.

"Everybody okay back there?" the driver asked.

"Tolerable," Monsignor Grace said. "That was an interesting ride, one I hope never to repeat. Sister Winifred, it's best we walk off all that jostling about."

"And Aggie's foot in my face."

"Sorry."

"You should be."

"You're alive, aren't you?"

She began patting her arms and shoulders. "Seems like it." Grinning, she threw her arms around me and hugged hard. "Thanks, but let's not do this again."

The driver got out and opened the door for the monsignor, then stuck his head back in to talk to me. "I need to check the car." I got out to help him. "You did good, Sister."

"So did you. What *is* your name?"

"Johnny Altieri, ma'am." He got the flashlight out of the glove box and looked under the middle section of the car.

"Seems okay under here." But the number of holes in the back and left side of the car was mute evidence of the intent of the men who had been shooting at us. "Shit! Seventeen hits."

Winnie sucked in her breath. "Seventeen hits. God have mercy!" The rosary was getting a workout tonight. By the time this case was over, she'd need a new one.

Johnny got down on the ground. He slid a bit under the car, and, using the flashlight to illuminate the underbelly, felt around under the car's rear and front fenders. When he brought his hand out it was coated with something sticky.

"What's that?"

"Brake fluid."

"Oooh, that's not good."

"We should be dead right now."

"Not possible. We have friends in high places." I pointed upward. "As high as they go."

"Well, we both have friends," Johnny said, also pointing, this time to a cream-colored Cord and blue Ford roadster that screeched into the parking lot.

Vincent rolled down the passenger-side window of the roadster. "Problems?"

"Just a few," I answered, pointing to the car. "In fact, seventeen nice round ones."

Richard bolted from the Cord to check out the bullet holes. He swore worse than my uncles did after a weekend wake. "How the hell?" He stomped over to Johnny, pulled at his shirt and jerked him close. "You better have a good explanation for this."

"Hey! It's not my fault. The car came out of nowhere."

I pulled at Richard's arm, but just as he'd done when we were kids, he easily shook me off. "Stop it, Richard! He did all he could. They even shot him."

"Yeah," Johnny said, "and then the sister took over."

"Took over?" He clenched on Johnny's shirt, drawing it

tighter, and glowered at him and then me. "What does he mean, you took over?"

"I got to shoot a gun. A big one."

Johnny had to talk between gritted teeth because his feet were nearly off the ground. "Took out both headlights. Left them blind."

Richard loosened his grip on Johnny's shirt and the man slumped to the ground, staggering to keep his balance. Richard turned to me. His gaze went everywhere—to the sky, to my torso, to my forehead, my brogans, my face. "Aggie . . . ah, Christ!" He pulled me to him and all I could register was the scent of sandalwood soap and a soupçon of fear. He hugged me hard, then let go and backed away. "So, brat, you're a hero."

"Heroine."

"Aggie . . ." Hands on knees, he bent over and sucked in dusty air. "Aggie . . ."

"It's okay, Richard. We didn't get killed. We're in one piece—except for Johnny and the car."

"Ah, yes," Vincent said. He slammed the door of the roadster, and took a look at Johnny's hand first, then his auto. "Well, it was time to get a new one."

Carlo checked out the car in almost the same way Johnny had. "They won't be able to get to Providence," he said.

I looked at the two vehicles and started to giggle. "There's not enough room for a flea in either of your cars, never mind the four of us."

"You can ride with me," Richard said. "Winnie has squeezed into the half seat before."

"Monsignor Grace, you're stuck with us," Vincent said. "You won't be as comfortable in Carlo's car as you were in the Lincoln, but at least you'll be able to get back to the city."

"What about Johnny?" I asked.

"There's a safe house a few miles from here. He can walk.

He's done it before."

"Safe house?"

"A place where we can go to ground when we need to," Carlo said.

"Oh." They were prepared for war at all times. What a way to live.

"I can't figure it out," Carlo said. "Why would they attack two nuns and a priest?"

"They didn't," I said. "They attacked Vincent's car, thinking he was in it."

"So it's escalated," Richard said.

Although Johnny started walking, Richard picked him up, and Winnie made room for him in the cramped back seat. We dropped him a few miles down the road and he waited until we got underway. The last I saw of him was a dark silhouette leaning against a tree.

"Why's he just standing there?"

"It wouldn't be a safe house if anyone other than the family knew where it was."

"After getting shot at, you'd think we'd *be* family."

"I'll mention it to Vincent. Maybe he'll adopt you like Donato did me." I gasped. "When my parents died, the old man took me in and later it seemed reasonable to adopt me."

"Holy moley. I never knew that."

"Well, it was after you moved to that big house off Elmwood Avenue. We only got to see each other in the summers after that—you at your grandmother's, me at mine. The things that happen to us in this life. Interesting, isn't it?"

"That's what you call it?"

"Don't worry, brat. I'm my own man."

The trip into the city was silent and gloomy as I pondered what Richard had told me. Winnie fell asleep and I didn't blame her. She hadn't signed on for this kind of misadventure when she joined the convent. Like most of the sisters, peace and quiet and a life given to prayer, service and worship were all she ever wanted. We had both chosen to be nuns for different reasons. Mine was mostly for independence and an education. Hers was a promise she had made to the Blessed Mother. That's the way she always told it—that she had promised if she got a date for the prom that she would join the convent. It was a good story, but I'd never be convinced that it was the only reason. No one joined the convent for something that frivolous. The Lord didn't expect us to give up a normal life if that was what our hearts desired. My wanting to be educated and independent meant I would have to subjugate myself to the will of the Lord, the hierarchy of the Church, and to a series of Mother Superiors, rules, and deprivation. If it was truly independence I wanted, I wouldn't find it in the convent. No matter how much I kicked against the traces, broke the rules, asserted my will, I knew I was bound to my Lord, and I was content in that.

I just had to stay alive to enjoy it.

"Aggie?"

"Yes, Richard?"

"Don't do that again."

I knew what he meant and why he said it. He worried about me. "I didn't start it."

"Maybe you should bow out of this and let Vincent handle it."

"I might, but now I'm mad as a wet cat. They shot at me, Richard. I must admit it was fun to shoot those lights out, but I was scared. Not because I might die. I'm prepared for that. But because I might not be able to stop them." A thought occurred to me, one I'd never had before, but had been in my thoughts since his surprising revelation. "Is that what it's like for you?"

"Me? Why would you think I'd know anything about that?"

"Well, you're part of the family, so you must do work for Vincent."

"I choose to honor my father's sense of right and wrong. I'm Dante's driver and bodyguard. That's all. I don't get involved in anything else. Ever."

"You've never been shot at?"

"Not unless you count the two years I spent in the Army, but the bullets were shot over our heads."

Oh, thank God! "It's an interesting experience, isn't it?"

"Yeah."

"We have a lot to do tomorrow."

"I suppose."

"If they were willing to kill Vincent, they've stopped trying to hide their objective. We may not be able to avert a war, but we have to try."

"Why can't you back off, Aggie?"

"Because Dante . . ."

"Asked you to help. I know. But now that it's come to this, you could get out and no one would blame you. You're a nun, for Christ's sake."

"I'm Dante's last hope of settling this peaceably." I stared out at the bright lights and noticed that we were on Elmwood Avenue, only a few blocks away from the convent and my old home. I'd tried to get away but had made almost a complete circle. As Richard had said: life was interesting. "I'd like to talk to Donato Ricci tomorrow."

"I'm not sure that can be arranged."

"Arrange it, Richard."

"You won't stop, will you?"

"I can't. I want to be the one to find out who tried to kill me by mistake."

I expected the convent to be dark when we arrived, but one of the rooms was blazing with light.

132

"Oh, blast!"

"Problems?"

"Mother Frances is keeping late hours."

"I brought some good beef and pork for the nuns. Maybe she'll let you off easy."

Sure. And pigs flew. Today Winnie had discovered a murder. I'd seen a girl die. We'd both been shot at with real bullets by very bad guys. Yet none of this was as scary as what was waiting for me in Mother Frances' office. Mother Frances.

CHAPTER TWELVE

It was Sister Rosalia on duty that night. I rang the bell and she whipped open the door.

"Oh, we've been so worried!" Her eyes rounded and she gasped. "Sister Winifred, what happened to your face?"

"Sister Agnes happened," Winnie said.

The lights illuminated a large black shoe polish mark on Winnie's face and a red patch right next to her eye in the shape of a brogan's heel. "Oh, Winnie, I'm so sorry."

"It's nothing, Aggie."

"You haven't seen it," Sister Rosalia said.

Winnie linked her arm in mine. "We're still here, my friend. That's all that matters."

I gave the parcel of beef and pork to Rosalia and told her to expect a large shipment early in the morning. "Bed for us. It's been a long day and we do have early Mass tomorrow."

Rosalia slammed the ice box door and touched my shoulder. "Bed for Sister Winifred, but Mother Frances wants to see you in her office immediately."

"Blast!"

"Aggie, I can come with you," Winnie offered.

"You're exhausted and hurt. I've been on the carpet before this. I'll probably be on the carpet after this. It's okay. What can she do? Fire me?"

It was something we talked and, yes, often joked about, we long-term sisters—that even in this horrible Depression we were secure in our calling, in our faith, in our very lives. We were well fed while others were starving, which is why we set up our soup line—to give back. We were comfortably housed in large buildings, when others had been evicted from tiny apartments, forced to live on the streets. Hence the reason for the small parish shelter two blocks away. We lived purposeful lives in service to our Lord, while others lost their jobs and drifted in disbelief and daily fear, their faith shattered along with their hope.

Hope. *I* hoped Mother Frances wouldn't send me to the wilds of Exeter with its subfreezing winters and mosquito-laden summers. She had threatened it often enough; but we both knew she hadn't the authority to send me anywhere. Only the Mother House could do that, and so far, because of pressure from Monsignor Grace, the Chancery had seen fit to leave Winnie and me right here. We were poor Mother Frances' trials and tribulations—in more ways than one.

I didn't have to knock on her office door. It was wide open. She was there, at her desk, reading the New Testament. Wait a minute! It was upside down. Oh mercy, I was in real trouble.

As she had taught each of us, I stood there on the other side of the threshold, waiting for her to acknowledge me. Independence, my left foot!

She beckoned to me. "Shut the door." She indicated the chair in front of her. Darn my socks! If I had to sit, it was going to be a long audience. "There was a message waiting for me when I returned," she said. "Monsignor Grace's work, I've no doubt."

What did she expect me to say? I didn't even know who had sent the message or what it was about. "Was it?"

"Do you dispute it?"

"I don't know what *it* is."

"You are a source of deep sorrow to me, Sister."

"I know. I wish it weren't so."

"Yet you continue this madness of poking your nose into *things* I have always thought would sully the very habit you wear."

"Children being held against their will by human monsters and young girls dying from poison are not *things*, Mother. Those victims are God's children, and they need our help."

"Sister Agnes, they *have* help—the Providence police and your very competent cousin. When class is in session, your pupils need your help. They need you to teach them the blessings of the Church. And here at the convent you have your daily duties and responsibility to God."

"Is that what the message said? That I should stop?"

"You know it didn't."

"No, I don't know."

"You and Sister Winifred are being excused from your duties." She sighed as if the whole world was pressing down on her. Maybe her world was. "I've never heard of such a thing happening." She fiddled with the pages of the New Testament and then very deliberately shut it. Bracing her hands on her desk, she slowly rose. "If I appeal, I will be reprimanded. If I allow this to happen, I will break all the vows I took when I was anointed as a Mother Superior. My duty is to instruct you in the ways of this order, to uphold the spirit of the Lord within you, to keep you from sin, to make you ready to be with the Lord in heaven. How can I do that and still sit by while you traipse around with Vincent Ricci?"

"I don't traip—"

"Silence!" She sucked in her breath, closed her eyes for a moment, and shook her head. When she opened her eyes, all she said was, "Please."

Please? As she got up and walked around her desk, I held my tongue and my breath. It seemed to me that what she had said came from a place she rarely went, from a pain she had forgotten she could feel. Did she count herself a failure? She had not been able to make me a perfect nun. Not even close. How awful for her to feel so helpless, to feel as if she were losing a soul to sin. *It must be killing her, Lord.*

"I've requested a week at the Mother House. Will that be enough for you to conclude your . . . your work?"

"Mother, you don't need to . . ."

"What I need is to bury myself in prayer. A retreat will help me get some peace. Perhaps in deep prayer the Lord will explain what is happening and why." She walked behind me and I heard her stop in front of the portrait of St. Catherine. "She was a maverick, you know . . . St. Catherine."

"Yes, Mother."

"She stood up for what she believed. She chastised and instructed the Pope on matters usually debated and decided only by the cardinals. He held her in such high esteem that he made her a doctor of the Church. A maverick, a woman maverick, became one of the highest authorities in the Church. Imagine." It took supreme will not to jump when she put her hands on my shoulders. "Are you *our* maverick, Sister Agnes?"

"I'm just a nun, Mother."

"But not the perfect nun."

"No."

"Do you remember the lessons you were taught before you were confirmed? The ones that teach us that there was and is only one perfect being?"

"Christ."

"For a long time now, I have forgotten those lessons."

Oh, dear Lord! She's in such pain. What can I do? But that's so little! All right, whatever You say.

With the knowledge that it was so little but so right, with only my fingertips I touched her hands.

She grasped my fingers, let them go and rounded her desk.

She looked at me for a long moment, then her face changed. It wasn't much of a smile but at least it wasn't a grimace or glare.

"We're going to be all right, you and I," she said. "You will let me know when you've completed your investigation?"

"Yes, Mother."

"I will be gone when you awaken. Sleep well, Sister Agnes."

"And you, Mother Frances."

"You may go."

"Mother . . ."

"Not now, Sister. Let's wait until I return."

"Yes, Mother."

As I wearily trudged up the stairs to my cell, my head pulsed and whirled. What just happened? At first her behavior made me think that she was angry with me. That wasn't possible, though, or we wouldn't have left each other on that hopeful note. Winnie wasn't going to believe it happened. I didn't believe it happened.

What a night!

The next day Richard picked us up right after the six a.m. Mass, and after I'd had time to call Mrs. Vandergelder, who had been only too happy to help. Her driver and two bodyguards were on their way when Richard pulled up outside the convent. He was driving a brand-spanking-new brown Model A Ford, one a lot more comfortable for Winnie than his Cord was. "Just came off the showroom floor," he said to me. "The manager was happy to open up at dawn for Vincent. Why wouldn't he be? Vincent always buys the best. Everything's automatic and it can reach eighty miles an hour."

"I do *not* want a demonstration."

He laughed. "I thought you were a big, bad nun. If you can shoot headlamps out of commission, why are you afraid of a little speed?"

"Forty miles an hour is a little speed. Eighty is suicide."

"Don't worry. I won't go eighty. I promised I'd keep you in one piece, and just in case someone else has other ideas, Vincent sent us a backup."

"We're being followed?"

"Yep."

"Just like *Public Enemy.*" I giggled. "The only gangster film I've ever seen and I'm right in the middle of a reenactment of the screenplay."

"Your life is a screenplay," Winnie said. *"I'm No Angel."*

"Winnie, we wear binders on our . . . uh . . . chest. How can you think I look and act like Mae West?"

"Don't be silly. Cary Grant."

I huffed while she and Richard laughed uproariously.

"I don't know," Richard sputtered. "I think her life is more like *Monkey Business.*"

"Now, I'm a Marx brother!"

"Or the monkey!"

"Go ahead, both of you, laugh. I'll just get me some new best friends."

Winnie giggled and patted my head. "No one will have you, Aggie. Bullets and bad guys are not exactly the kinds of things that would endear you to a new best friend."

"What a boring life my new best friend must live."

"Don't worry, brat," Richard said, "you and your life are endearing to us. We're not going anywhere."

"I'm so glad. I couldn't do without you both."

The landscape changed, but not the way I expected it to. It should have been winding lanes, a few farms and a big lake surrounded by tall pine trees. We got winding lanes, but they led to straighter roads and lots of houses clustered in small neighborhoods. "I thought we were going to Wallum Lake."

"That's what Vincent wants people to think—that his father is in the sanitarium. He's not."

"Then where is he?"

"Warwick Neck. Donato is being treated privately in a boathouse he rented on the Aldrich Estate. He has round-the-clock nurses and a doctor on the premises."

"In a boathouse?"

"It has gilt molding, crystal chandeliers in every room, thick Turkey rugs, silk sheets and a gourmet Italian chef. Most of all, Donato has quiet, cool, recuperative salt air and a great view of Narragansett Bay."

"Wow," Winnie said. "Nice what money can buy."

"Money and power," I said.

"That, too."

The foyer smelled of white flour paste, probably from the pristine blue and white toile wallpaper, flocked here and there with velvet. The floors were slate with a deep blue rug that was so thick it could only be woolen. Just inside was a set of oak winding stairs that hugged the walls on two sides. Mounted on the wall were photos and portraits, most of faraway places and times long past. On examination, I noted the fading photos of gentlemen with grey tweed coats and matching caps, great mustaches, rather sloppy pants, and a few rifles slung over their shoulders. The women wore black, mostly, with aprons and head scarves. Some carried market baskets, others held babies in their arms, with one or two children clutching their skirts. The buildings were those I'd seen in travel books of Europe, and I could easily recognize a spire in the distance that bespoke an Italian village. It wasn't surprising. Donato had wanted a taste of home. Here, in what might be his last home, he had surrounded himself with the memories of it, too. At the very top of the stairs, just before an open door, was a framed oil painting of a very modern version of a coat of arms. I recognized it as the same one that had come on the invitation to Catherine's Memorial Mass. A cap dominated the top of the arms, as

Vincent's had. But this one showed a knife lying on its side right under the cap. Below, separated by a cross and bar were a chicken on the left and three fleur de lis on the right.

I stared at the crest for a moment, once more struck by that chicken and its companions on the shield. From a lesson on castles and knights we'd had just before the Christmas recess, I remembered that early coats of arms and heraldic shields were at first war identifications, meant to be seen across a field of battle so the participants didn't kill the wrong person. They had quickly turned into family crests indicating the history of a family, and could be read like a story. This, I supposed, was the story about the Ricci family.

Ruminating on what the shield or coat of arms meant to convey, I didn't pay much attention to where we were going until we entered a room bathed in light, where huge windows looked out on the surf crashing on rocks, casting spray in the air, wetting the seagulls that playfully darted into and out of the droplets.

I shifted away from the delightful scene to the man who could command such beauty.

Even propped in a bed, Donato Ricci was imposing. His grey hair and rather rakishly thick mustache gave him the appearance of a swashbuckling pirate. His breathing, however, told a different story. Each breath was wet and labored. No wonder the bad guys weren't after him. He looked like he could die at any minute.

CHAPTER THIRTEEN

After he said, "Welcome," he coughed, winced, and sucked in hard on a big black mask to get enough oxygen to continue.

My Uncle Tom had had such a cough before he died, drowning in an ocean in his lungs. Having nursed him for several months, I knew what to do and leaned over so Mister Ricci and I were within inches of each other. "Whisper. It's easier to whisper and then breathe that cold air. When it gets too much, let me know and I'll help you with the oxygen. Besides, whatever we say will be just between us. Those other two don't have to hear a thing."

"You will tell?"

"Not a word. On my honor."

"Ah!" He breathed gently for a time, then reached a shaky hand up to touch my cheek with calloused fingertips. "Too pretty to be a nun."

"Yet, I am."

"The nun who will solve this mystery?" He sounded incredulous.

"The nun who wants to try."

"So you've come to me."

"I believe in starting at the top."

"Ah, courtesy. Not many have it these days." He coughed harder than the last time, and it took several deep inhalations of the oxygen before he had enough energy to speak again. When he could, he asked, "What can I do for you, Sister?"

"Tell me about the shield."

"That's all?"

"Do I need more than that?"

He might be a sick man but his keen gaze was sharp as a man half his age. I could see the calculations zipping through his mind. *How much can I tell her? How much to leave out? What will help Vincent and Dante? What might get my family in trouble later?* His eyes flashed, and then for the first time he showed more than bravado. Well, actually, less. Surprisingly, there was a softening there and I hoped for the best.

A half hour later, we took our leave of one of the most powerful and feared men in Rhode Island, who was now hooked up to a portable oxygen pump, unable to move about without pain. Power? This end was about as powerless as anyone could get.

"Did he give you what you came for?" Richard asked.

"I got a nice story. I'm just not sure what part of it to believe."

"That's Donato. Vincent always said that he kept his plans and reasons for them to himself. Where others have *consiglieri*, he has his genius mind. Ever since I was a kid, Donato's steely stare gave me the willies. It felt as if he was seeing right through my skin."

"Yes, I had the same feeling."

"Where to next?"

"Lunch, I think. On the Hill."

"One of Vincent's restaurants?"

"Not today. We don't get out much and I want to get the flavor of the Hill, maybe talk to a few people. Pizza okay, Winnie? Or should we eat our way through the cheese store?"

"Not cheese. Spinach pie from Venda's," Winnie suggested. "Can we afford it?"

"They'll put it on Vincent's chit," Richard said. "Shall we get some dessert for the other sisters?"

"Apian Way's rice pie with almond-flavored whipped cream?"

I had to stifle a laugh. Winnie was absolutely salivating. "Yes, let's. Sister Noble can cut it into small pieces."

Richard didn't bother to conceal his disbelief. "One pie? I think Vincent would be willing to spring for two or three pies for the good sisters."

Federal Hill was bustling with cars and people. The cars were parked at crazy angles, sometimes blocking in other cars and delivery trucks, a few backed wheels up onto the small sidewalk, where supplies for the dozen or so pushcarts could be off-loaded. Richard pulled into an alleyway circling behind Capodimonte Ristorante, one of the best Tuscan-style restaurants on the Hill.

"Vincent's place?"

"One of them," Richard said.

A young man in a brown suit pushed open the screen door in the back of the restaurant, saw who had parked, smiled and saluted Richard. He went back into the restaurant but soon returned, folding chair in hand, set it up next to the car and sat down, pulling a softcover book out of his pocket. "Have a nice day," he said.

I hit Richard on the arm. "I can't believe it. Even your car gets a bodyguard."

"Perks."

"You mean tentacles."

"Same thing."

I stopped and sniffed. "Oh, my Lord!" I was overcome by the tantalizing smells coming out of the first pushcart—roasted peppers and Italian sausage. And Winnie wanted spinach pies!

Richard—who had always been tuned into my thoughts and appetites—nudged me. "Want a snack?"

I sneaked a peek at him and, of course, found him grinning as broadly as that young boy I'd grown up with. Except for the mustache. It was beginning to look less dreadful. Someday I might actually like it. Right now, however, I was hungry. I held my thumb and index finger about two inches apart.

"Two shorties, Stefano," he told the man stirring the peppers. "No, make that three."

He gave Winnie and me the small hot sandwiches and popped his own into his mouth. Biting off a tiny corner, I savored the fennel bite of the sausage and the soft, slightly charred flavor that the pepper gave to it. As I took the final bite, Richard held out a quarter to Stefano, who waved it away and then turned his back so Richard couldn't insist.

"More perks?"

Richard shook his head and pushed the quarters underneath the towel Stefano had been using. In front of a pizza parlor, Richard said, "Stefano is proud. I floated him a loan when he lost his job at a jewelry factory, when they let Italians go immediately, no matter what their jobs. He paid it back a long time ago, but he still won't take any money from me."

"So you have to sneak it."

"He'll put it in his pocket and then put it in the collection basket this Sunday. He's good people, Aggie."

"I'm sure he is."

I was pretty sure I was surrounded by more good people in this colorful part of Providence. We walked a half block under the many awnings that shaded the sidewalk, dodging cats and dogs, running children, and harried parents chasing them down. Mothers came out of Coletti's clothing store, where everyone shopped for First Communion dresses. Fathers led their children into the grocery store or stopped to buy them colorful ices or candy sweets from other pushcart vendors. Old and young were gathered around pushcarts with signs that read *Whipple Avenue Cooperative* or some Italian phrase I couldn't translate, but was probably much like the others. Each was heaped with home-garden fruits and vegetables selling for five cents a pound, butter and eggs on ice for eight cents.

But other mothers and fathers, eyes vacant or hurting, stood at corners or next to store entrances with their hands out, begging for something that would get them through that day and the next. Richard gave each of them a quarter. Judging from the signs in the pushcarts' price lists or the store windows, they could get a pound of chicken, enough vegetables for a family of four, bread and a gallon of milk with that quarter.

"Vincent feeds them at soup kitchens. You do it this way."

"It isn't important how we do it. We just have to do it."

"Yes. Thank you." I tucked my arm into his and hugged my friend.

"Venda's," Winnie said.

The tiny shop was crowded—well, it could only hold about half a dozen comfortably—but there were at least that many pushing up against the counter. Venda's was the place to get homemade pasta and other Italian specialties. The glass-enclosed counter had hand-lettered signs indicating what was in the steel containers. That day there were jumbo stuffed shells, manicotti, three different colors and flavors of linguini, tortellini, lasagna and ravioli. Most of those begging outside would faint at the sight of this kind of food. But we were here for something less exotic, more earthy—a crisp baked bread pocket stuffed with well-cooked spinach, bits of pepperoni sausage, hot red pepper flakes and ricotta or mozzarella cheese. The pockets came hot from the oven or already baked and cold from a night on ice.

Winnie ordered a cold one. I got mine steaming hot. Richard opted for the jumbo stuffed shells. They came in pressed paper containers, and we took them into the small courtyard a block away where there were benches for just this purpose—eating, the thing Italians loved best to do. Everyone there had some kind of foodstuff in their hands, most going into their mouths. I had to blow on my choice before I got one bite, while Winnie was already halfway through hers.

Winnie stretched, then leaned over to ask me, "Are you going to tell us what Donato said, or are you going to make us wonder?"

A woman carrying two large canvas market bags stopped in front of us. I recognized her as the mother of Eugenio Carcieri—my student who had mimicked a gargoyle . . . was it only two days ago? Like all the Italians I knew, once introduced, you were family; and family was entitled to break into any "family" conversation. I had become used to it over the years, so I wasn't surprised when Eugenio's mother asked, "You talked to Donato Ricci, Sister Agnes?"

"Why, hello, Mrs. Carcieri. How are you?"

"Fine. And so is Eugenio. The whole family is fine. I hope Signore Ricci is also fine?"

"Of course" *All, right, Lord. No lies. But how about a simple evasion? I did promise Donato. Uh, yes, You're right; the promise didn't include a description of his health, so perhaps it won't hurt.* "Actually, he's quietly enduring the ordeals of his illness."

"Did he tell you if he's coming back to Providence? We all miss him and hope he will be well enough to visit the neighborhood."

"I don't think he could walk without pain, Mrs. Carcieri. What he's hoping is that his treatments will give him the strength to visit with his sons and grandson in his own home."

"Oh, dear. I was so hoping that he'd be able to make a stop in our shop. My husband supplied him with cigars. Did you know that? He's still holding on to an old box for him."

"I don't think he'd be able to enjoy them now."

"That's too bad. He did like his occasional cigar. He and his friends used to come in to check on that box every so often. But now that they're dying off, no one has been in for a while.

Perhaps you could tell him that we—my husband, that is—is still taking good care of the box for him and ask him what he'd like us to do with the cigars?"

I couldn't imagine that Donato would care much about an old box of cigars, but she was so concerned that he be told they were still doing their duty by him, that I had to set her mind at ease. "I'd be happy to."

When she took her leave, Richard tugged on my sleeve and leaned over to whisper, "Look around slowly. They're all staring at us."

He was right. People stared; a few rose and went to someone close, said something, and then they both turned to stare. "What's going on?"

"Damned if I know."

Winnie finished her last bite. "It's you, of course, ninny."

"Oh, please, Winnie! There can't be more than two people who know me and one of them just left."

"Well, why else would we be getting this much notice? Most people either ignore nuns or don't even see them."

That was true. A nun could walk into a room, mingle and then leave and it was as if she had never been there. It was something about the habit. In a state where Catholics dominated the population, we were so familiar we made no impact. But these staring eyes and unconcealed whispers were very unusual. They were making me uncomfortable. "Let's go. We need to get the pies at Apian Way and I want to speak to Vincent before we go back to the convent."

Within two minutes I knew what a movie star felt like—or a quail at hunting season. The staring people circled us. I stayed really close to Richard, just in case. But then I noticed that they were all smiling, thank goodness. One by one, they touched me or tilted their caps or dropped a curtsy as if I were royalty! Each asked to be remembered to Donato. Donato, the just. Donato, the savior of the poor. Donato, the friend of children.

"He always had a kind word, Sister."

"He always knew our names."

"My mother knew him in the old country. She said when he became Signore Capo, they could breathe again. Would you give him her regards the next time you see him?"

"Of course. What's her name?"

"Josephine. Josephine Cardi."

"He always had a pocket full of change for the children."

"I was in the children's home right after the Great War. I didn't have a coat. Seventeen others didn't, either. Signore Don got all of us warm coats and gloves and hats. None of us got the influenza. He did that, saved us."

"My mother needed an operation and she couldn't pay for it. I don't know how he did it, but she got her operation. She died two months ago, twenty-two years after the doctors told her to go home and prepare to die."

"In the old country, my uncle disappeared one day. The *banditti* had him and his two children. They even took my mother. They wanted a ransom, but my family was poor. Even if all the sisters and brothers pooled their money, it wouldn't be enough. One of my cousins was dumped dead on his doorstep for his sainted mother to find. My mother won't talk about that time in the hills with the *banditti*, except to say that Signore Ricci tracked down the captors and rescued all of them. Tell him he is always in the Beltri family's prayers."

"My father was out of work for three months. Signore Capo talked to his boss and my father got his job back, with a raise."

"Tell him we miss him."

"Tell him I'm praying for him."

"Tell him . . . tell him . . . tell him . . ."

By the time we got out of there, I was numb. "Who is Donato, Richard?"

"Who is anyone?"

"Sinner and saint. Gangster and generous fairy godfather. Two halves of one soul. It's mind-boggling."

We picked up the rice pies; Richard insisted we get three of them. On the way out he spied a huge tray of wedding cookies and bought them, too. *For the soup line.* I wasn't sure there was any sinner in his being. *What do You mean I can't discern the truth yet, Lord? I only have to suspend disbelief and look below the surface. He doesn't fail any criteria. Ooofah! Okay, You're the judge.*

We hadn't attracted enough attention in the little park. Noooo! So we went ahead and turned heads on the rest of the Hill—two nuns carrying a tray of wedding cookies. I wanted to shout out, "Brides of Christ," but wondered if anyone would know what that meant, especially to us.

When the guy in the brown suit saw us coming, he hurried to take the tray from us. "Are your arms shaking, Winnie?" I asked.

"Like gelatin. How heavy was that?"

"I'd guess they weighed about what the pies do. Fifteen pounds," Richard said.

"Boy, are we out of shape."

"Richard, Antonio took a call for you. He said to tell you that you should call a Monsignor Grace. He's trying to find you and the sisters. The number is on the cork board."

"I'll be right back," Richard said. He pointed to the brown suit. "Watch them like your own mother, Tony. If anybody you don't know turns that corner, hold your gun on him and give me a shout."

"You bet!"

"Oh, no you don't, Richard!" Winnie said. "We've had enough of gun business. We're going with you."

"Suit yourself."

The back door led to the kitchen, where dozens of people were preparing meals. I spied polenta being stirred and poured onto large cookie sheets, to be slid onto shelves in a large cold room. Chicken and lamb aromas made my mouth water. And the bread! Round, crusty bread. Black square loaves. The traditional split-top Italian. At least a half dozen other shapes, sizes and flavors, from rye to sesame.

"Stop gawking, Aggie," Winnie said. "It's only food."

"Just like a Monet is only oil paint and canvas."

Richard took us into a small office next to a storeroom. He picked a note off a cork board, read it, picked up the telephone and asked the operator to connect him with the number he read off the note. Within a few minutes he said hello to Monsignor Grace, then passed the phone to me.

"Sister Agnes?"

"Yes, Monsignor."

"We need to talk. Here. At the Chancery."

"Yes, Your Eminence?"

"About the murders."

"We already did."

"No, not Catherine or Kitty. The other three."

CHAPTER FOURTEEN

It was a never-ending nightmare. After we dropped off the milk-and-egg-laden rice pies and wedding cookies at the convent, we high-tailed it to the Chancery. The quiet of the Chancery belied the amount of activity behind all those closed doors: clacking of typewriter keys, ringing of telephones, echoes of running footsteps—all in the service of the Church.

Monsignor Grace welcomed us into his office, where a complete coffee service was waiting. I had been bouncing in the seat all the way here, my anxiety level and heartbeat higher than ever.

I put one foot over the threshold and all but demanded, "What do you mean, the other three? Are Vincent and Dante all right?"

"As far as I know, yes. I didn't call you about them." He waved his assistant over to pour coffee or tea for each of us, waited while we fixed it, then dismissed the young curate with a shooing motion of his hand. "It's been bothering me since yesterday."

Oh, I was not in the mood for evasions or long drawn out stories. Monsignor Grace was, well, gracious and endearing, but too much is too much. "Who else was murdered?"

"I don't know for certain, but I think Donato's associates were."

"His associates?"

Richard leaned toward the monsignor. "You mean Donato's *partners?*"

"Yes. Tiny's father and the Santini brothers."

Richard jolted back in his seat. "We were told that they died from geriatric complications."

"Yes, I know," Monsignor Grace said. "But what are geriatric complications? Lack of oxygen from lung problems? Could be smothering. Blood clot? Heart attack? If they died of either of those, wouldn't the death certificate say so? I had my assistant check the death certificates. None of them listed a specific cause of death. On each, just those exact words: geriatric complications. I called a couple of doctors at Rhode Island Hospital and the attending physician at the morgue. They are all Catholics and communicants here at the cathedral. I asked them point-blank if there was any indication that those deaths could have come from unnatural causes."

"And they said what?" I asked; but I had this gut feeling that I already knew the answer.

"To a man—and separately—they said some of the doctors at the hospital, including them, had had their suspicions at the times of the deaths, but the attending physicians might have been pressured into giving a sort of 'natural causes' diagnosis."

"Let me guess," I said. "Because if they didn't, there *might* be a war on the streets."

"Yes."

"Yes. Like what *might* have happened if Catherine's death hadn't been listed as accidental." I noticed that Winnie was once more saying her beads, this time quietly, thank goodness. "I'd like to know who made the final decision on Catherine's 'accident,' and if anyone exerted any pressure on him to pull away from a full investigation. The cops are not that stupid! We figured it out in less than half an hour, thanks to Winnie. They could have, too, but they didn't. Were they paid off? Were they urged off? Were they . . . Darn my socks! I don't know what could have induced them, but it must have been something big."

"Or someone," Winnie suggested.

"Yes, you're right, my friend. Some*one* important set this in motion. No matter what the reason, it will always come back to a person making a decision—and in this case it's beginning to look as if he didn't have altruistic motives. We have to find that person fast or there may be other deaths."

"Other unexplainable deaths," Monsignor Grace said. He sighed as if a heavy burden had descended on his shoulders.

For the first time I realized just what a burden it was to serve in this Diocese. His vocation demanded his absolute devotion to God and his flock. For a cleric, *Feed my sheep* is not just a metaphor. It's a heavenly commandment. And Monsignor Grace's flock included the saints and the sinners, the gangsters and the generous fairy godfathers, and everybody in between. He had to love them all, serve them all, guide them all, worry about them, pray for them, hear their childlike or hair-raising confessions, and absolve them of their sins if he determined that they were truly sorry. A heavy burden, indeed, for a man who cared; and Monsignor Robert Grace cared.

"I must talk to these attending physicians," I said.

"I prepared a list with their phone numbers and talked to a couple of them. But they don't have much information that will help. There were no post mortems, and the bodies won't yield anything after all this time. When the deaths occurred, each of them got a phone call—purportedly from Vincent's organization—asking them to spare the families more grief and to head off any gangland repercussions. They didn't want the hospital filling up with gunshot victims, and since the call supposedly came from Vincent, they each, on their own, agreed to keep their suspicions to themselves. One of them said that he did it because there was really no way for him to prove murder. 'It just looked funny,' he said. Sound familiar?"

"Catherine." I thought for a moment and got up to walk my thoughts into order. "You know, if it weren't for Dante, no one would have questioned Catherine's death. And if it weren't for Anna preparing the drinks tray instead of Ella, we wouldn't be on the hunt now. Kitty's death is the one thing that shows there is a conspiracy here. Yet her death isn't related to it."

"Isn't it?" Richard asked. "Do we know that for sure?"

"That depends on what Josiah and Monsignor Grace discover. Have you managed to get through to the Catholic authorities in Ireland?"

"I put in my calls, but the time difference probably is working against us. Plus, I had to chase down these doctors." He handed me a short list of names.

"Ah, one of these I recognize. He treats St. Catherine's nuns and priests."

"Dr. McMahon?" Winnie asked.

"The very one."

Winnie snorted. "He should be easy to pressure. Sister Rosalia turns on the tears and he wavers. I don't think she's ever had an injection."

"Easily manipulated? Right up your alley, Aggie," Richard said.

"It's his open clinic day. He should be there until five. Give us ten minutes and then could you call him, Monsignor?" He nodded. "Please tell him to let us in right away and that you want him to cooperate. Without your support, I'm not sure two lowly nuns and someone who works for Vincent will be enough ammunition to get him to tell more than the bare bones. He's going to want to save his reputation if all this comes out."

"Can we keep his and the others' names out of this if it does come out?" Richard asked. "Vincent is going to want some kind of justice and so will the others. These doctors say that they were trying to avoid an uproar; but their actions could very well precipitate it."

"Even if they cooperate?"

"I don't know. It will take you to intervene for them with Vincent. And Donato."

"You can count on me."

It was a good thing we had the monsignor's assurance, because Dr. McMahon would have loved to dismiss us after the initial introductions. He was nervous, watching the telephone as if it would ring at a mere wish, or jumping up to open the door if a noise sounded beyond it. Once, a fly buzzed into the screen and the slight ping induced a palsy-like movement of his hand and arm.

"I did what I was asked to do. It was the right thing at the time," he insisted.

I stared him down and he shrank into his high-backed leather chair. I pointed to his wall where a framed copy of the Hippocratic Oath was prominently displayed among his degrees and medical license. "What does that state? Do what you're asked to do? Or is it: *First do no harm?* This is about as much harm as anyone in the world could have done. Own up to it and help us find out what really happened to these men."

"Men? More than one?"

"Three, to be exact," Richard said.

"No, Richard. Three men, two women. So far. We're here to avoid a sixth death. Or maybe a dozen more if what you did gets out."

"Oh, my God!" The doctor drew out a monogrammed handkerchief and wiped his sweaty brow. "I was trying to *avoid* confrontation and more deaths."

"All you did was hide the truth. That can't be a good thing. Ever."

"I didn't know the truth. I only had my suspicions."

"Right. So you ignored the suspicions, and the influenza took hold until now the epidemic might attack us all."

Richard and Winnie both rolled their eyes and I got a tongue-lashing from on high. *Yes, Lord, I know that was a really dumb analogy, but I'm improvising as fast as I can. Maybe he won't notice. In any case, You could help out, You know! We're getting in a muddle, here. So stay close, okay?*

"He said he was speaking for Vincent and the family. He emphasized family, so I figured he really was from the *family*, you know?" Oh, boy! Now I wanted to roll my eyes, but I smiled and nodded. "He just said it would be better for everybody if the death was listed as geriatric complications."

"*He* said geriatric complications?"

"Yes."

"And you agreed?"

Now, he was squirming. "Yes."

"What are geriatric complications? And how did you get that euphemism past the medical examiner?"

"There wasn't a medical examiner. My patient—Amadeo Santini—died in the hospital. I signed the death certificate as I was told to do, and the hospital filed it with the city."

"It's that simple?"

"Of course. Everyone believes doctors."

"And doctors believe telephone calls, and now five people are dead."

"I didn't know."

"You didn't care, Dr. McMahon. You knew that what you were being asked to do was more than a little unusual, and that alone should have alerted you that something was wrong. You didn't care enough to make a simple phone call to Vincent himself, just to be certain that crazy call came from him. Or did the caller offer you some incentive to sign off on Giovanni's death? A payment or gift, perhaps?"

The sweat started flowing more freely. The handkerchief was going to be soaked. "I . . . I don't know what you're talking about. I was overworked. The request seemed reasonable at the time."

"I wonder if the licensing board will see it that way if this all comes out. I will pray for your immortal soul."

I was so angry that I slammed the door against the wall when I opened it. "What time is it?"

Richard checked his wristwatch. "Three thirty-seven. Why?"

"Geriatric complications. How many deaths are listed as geriatric complications, do you suppose? My Uncle Tom was eighty-nine when he died. There were four causes of death listed on his death certificate—everything from diabetes to acute alcohol poisoning, but not geriatric complications. I'd like to talk to some of the doctors at the hospital, find out what they think of that diagnosis."

"Let's do it by telephone."

"Sounds good to me."

"Me, too," Winnie said.

It might have sounded good, but it didn't work out that way. Every doctor we asked to talk to was busy. "He will call you back," we were told. They should have added, "When Jesus comes again, maybe."

"It's been forty minutes. This is a waste of time."

"Now, Aggie," Richard said. "A little patience."

"I have a better idea. There's a physician on duty twenty-four hours a day for Donato, isn't there?"

"That's right!"

"What kind of food does Donato like—something his gourmet Italian chefs won't make for him?"

"Chinese."

The forty-minute trip to Warwick Neck nearly undid us. The

aroma of soy sauce, ginger and garlic was too much even for the usually patient Winnie. The crackle-snap of paper alerted us to her sneaking a fried pork wonton from the container. Soon we were all chomping on the crusty, oily, exotic treats. It didn't matter. We had three more wonton orders and several entrees.

We pulled into the entrance to the Aldrich Estate as three other cars exited. Two sedans followed us, pulling into the driveway leading to the main house. Richard parked in the oval in front of the boathouse and led us to the front door, where he used his key to let us in. A housekeeper came to see what was happening, but Richard put his index finger to his lips and she smiled.

"He's going to smell the food," I whispered.

"Unless he's sleeping," Winnie said.

Richard stuck his head in the door. "Donato?" He stiffened, flung the door open and rushed forward.

"Good God!" Donato lay with his eyes closed, gasping. The oxygen apparatus was on the other side of the room, the mask dangling over the back of a chair. I dumped the food on a table and rushed to the oxygen. "Winnie, help me!" We struggled to move the great metal cylinder. "Richard!"

He rolled it instead of trying to pull it. "I thought this was supposed to have wheels on it!"

"It did this morning," I said.

Donato's lips were blue, as were the tips of his fingers. Richard turned the handle on the oxygen tank, and cold air *whoosh*ed out of the mask. I leaned over and put it against Donato's face. "Breathe," I said. "Breathe, please."

"God damn it! Where's the doctor?"

"Find him, Richard, please! I don't think this is working."

He rushed from the room and began flinging doors open. The housekeeper who had come into the front hall pounded up the stairs and into the room.

159

"*Dio mio!*"

"Where's the doctor?"

"*Dottore,* he go."

"Go where?"

"*Congedo!*"

"What?"

"He's been fired," Richard said.

"Who would do that?" Winnie asked.

"Who else?" Richard and I said together.

"The killer."

The housekeeper blanched and took up her rosary. She got down on her knees and prayed the beads, her head bowed.

"Richard!" I called. He rushed back to the bed. "He's panting. Richard, Uncle Tom did that right before . . ."

Richard leaned over and spoke directly into Donato's ear. "Don Ricci, don't you let the bastard win."

Donato opened his eyes and raised his hand to pat Richard's cheek. He sucked hard on the oxygen, and with a huge effort, pulled the mask off.

"No!" I shouted.

He smiled and touched his index finger to my forehead, then moved his hand to point twice out the door. His hand fumbled for the mask, then fell limp on top of it. He took one last weak breath, closed his eyes, and it was over.

CHAPTER FIFTEEN

"You call Vincent," I told Richard. "I'll call Monsignor Grace."

It took them an hour to get there, but as soon as they arrived, the boathouse became command central. Monsignor Grace gave Donato extreme unction while Vincent paced, swearing under his breath. Carlo held the candle and Winnie and I said the responses that might gain Donato a place in a heaven he believed in but might not qualify for. Only God knew whether there would be a welcoming or a banishing, but we were bound to try to save his soul even now, because we didn't know when or if it was too late.

When Monsignor Grace blew out the candle and put his sacred garments and vessels away, Vincent went to his father's side. *"Vendetta,"* he said.

"No!"

"Sister Agnes, stay out of this," he said. "You don't understand what this means."

"I do. So did he." I explained what Donato had done.

Vincent looked stricken. "He took off the mask? Richard, you saw this?"

"She's telling you the truth, Vincent. He took off the mask himself."

"He did more than that," I said. "He gave me a quest."

"What the hell are you talking about?"

"He wants . . . wanted . . . no, *wants* me to search for the truth."

Carlo snorted and shook his head. "He wouldn't do that. He knows our organization can do this without you."

"He did it." I explained the last act of Donato's life.

"What the hell does it mean?"

"I don't know yet. He obviously thinks there's something in my head that will help solve this. I need a little time to figure out what it is." My heart was beating a military tattoo in my chest. *Parum-pum-pum-Parum-pum-pum-Parum-pum-pum.* Only really fast. So fast, it was hard to catch my breath. "Wait two days, Vincent, please. Today is Thursday. If I can't put all the pieces together by six o'clock Saturday night, I'll turn it over to you."

"Well, we might be able to go along with that," Carlo said. "It will take that long to get our forces ready."

"Oh, no! Don't do that." I put my hands out in supplication. It was all I could do. *Lord, help me get through to this man.* "Please, Vincent, do nothing. Do nothing that will alert your enemy that you are coming for him. Him? He's still a ghost! You don't yet know who he is. So, please, please, please give me a chance. Don't get an arsenal together. Don't send anyone to safe houses. Don't enlist other families in your, um, plans. Mourn your father. Hold a wake. See who comes and who doesn't. Assess the mourners. Keep quiet about what happened here. Help your son understand the death of his grandfather, his *Nonno.* Honor your father's last request by letting me think. Isn't that what Donato would have done in your place?"

Carlo's spitting-angry gaze shifted to Vincent's and they both looked at the figure on the bed, the shrunken form of a man who was still loved by his sons and the people he had helped. And obviously hated by a worm who had tunneled into and begun to destroy the organization he had created.

Vincent asked that unmoving body, "What would you do, Don Ricci? Papa?" He picked a piece of lint off the bedspread.

"What should I do?"

"Prepare for war," Carlo said.

"And who do we fight, brother? Name him."

"We take them all down. If we do that, we get him."

"Them? Him? This bastard is in the family. *Our* family."

"That's not possible."

"There's no other explanation." Vincent brushed his father's hair back from his forehead, where it had been crushed by the mask. He looked up sadly at his brother. "Sister Agnes is right. He—our enemy, the killer of my wife and our father—is a ghost. A snake who probably smiles at us each day and plots to take over what is not rightfully his. We need to find him before we can fight him. Meanwhile, we close ranks. Only those in this room—and the devil who did this—know what really happened here. We must keep it that way while Monsignor Grace prepares a Funeral Mass for Monday. Robert, will the bishop allow us to use the cathedral?"

"I'll petition him; but I have no doubt he'll say yes."

"Remind him that half of Rhode Island might want to come to pay their last respects."

"I will."

"The wake should be three days—tomorrow, Saturday, Sunday." He bent to kiss his father on his cheek. "Sister, you have three days. Use them well."

"Thank you, Vincent."

"*Don* Vincenzo," Carlo said, and left the room.

"Don Vincenzo, may I speak with you?"

Vincent sent me a grimace of a smile. "Vincent is my name, Sister Agnes. What do you want?"

I walked him to the side, near the windows. "Carlo."

"He's young, hot-headed and angry right now, but he will mellow and come around."

"Not in time, I'm afraid." I touched his arm and felt the steel that was there—and hoped to God that I could melt it a little. "He is so angry that I'm afraid he may inadvertently say something to the wrong person, perhaps to that man-snake in your family."

"What do you have in mind?"

"Send him to the Franciscan Center. He'll have to exchange his college duds for a scratchy brown dress and rope belt, but if he's there, Dante will have his uncle with him to help him deal with his sorrow. And Carlo won't want to scare his nephew with wild talk."

"You don't think I should bring Dante home?"

"No! He could still be a target. We have to protect him at all costs. Carlo and the bodyguards can do that." A thought illuminated another possibility. "Although . . . we could sneak Dante into the funeral parlor on Sunday night in a big box among a dozen others in a shipment of flowers. That way, he can visit with his *Nonno* alone. Winnie and I can be there, if you think that will help."

"It would. But what if you're seen?"

"No one sees nuns, Vincent. We blend into the crowd during the day and are invisible in the night."

"Not with that bib of yours."

"A little black scarf will fix that."

"Good plan, Sister Agnes."

"Well, there's one other thing."

"There always is with you."

"I can alert Mrs. Vandergelder that no one except Carlo be allowed to talk to Dante or get anywhere close to him. The brothers know that, for good reasons, they can't admit that Dante is there. But we already know that this man-snake has impersonated you several times, and we can't let that happen with Dante. So Carlo must be on his guard constantly."

"He will be. But what do you mean the man-snake imperson-ated me?"

"Oh! I didn't have time to tell you what we found out!" I outlined everything we'd learned that day. "Richard can inform Tiny."

"I'll do that."

"I don't know the sons of the other partners, but they should be told."

"I'll take care of it all, but after the funeral. They haven't been in on this from the beginning. I'm not sure who's doing this. I hate to think it might be one of them, but right now I don't trust my own shadow."

"The tone of your voice . . . you're beginning to scare me."

"I want to kill the bastard. Slowly. Painfully."

"Vincent!"

"He killed my wife; my father; three old, old men; and one young girl. He's scum and should be flushed down the sewer in little pieces."

"You promised to let the police and me handle it."

"I promised not to start a war." He spun on his heel and started for the door. "I'm keeping my promise for three more days. After that, if you haven't unmasked this traitor, God help anyone who gets in my way."

"I will pray for you," Monsignor Grace told Vincent.

"Unless you find this man-snake, pray for the city, Robert."

He left, and we all realized that the mantle had passed. I only hoped that Vincent and Carlo could contain themselves until I had this figured out.

When I heard the front door slam, I pulled Monsignor Grace aside. "You're not thinking that Donato committed suicide, are you?"

"Of course not. Didn't he pull that mask off to tell you something?" I nodded. "He died before he could voice it, but you were all aware that that was his intention, correct?"

"Yes, Your Eminence."

"Then we will let the Lord sort it out."

The next hour was a blur of activity. The undertaker arrived to collect Donato's body. Monsignor Grace accompanied the casket, making a really small cortege. The housekeeper and two maids arrived with buckets and brooms, disinfectant and polish. Winnie and I shooed them away to astonished mutterings.

Richard laid out the cold Chinese food on plates he found on Donato's shelves. "Eat," he ordered.

"I'm not hungry."

"Eat. We can talk while we eat. And you can tell us what we have to do next."

"I don't know what we have to do next."

"Then eat and think, damn it!"

I nibbled on a few crispy noodles and tried to decipher that last confounding act of Donato's. Before I knew it, I was digging into the container of chicken chow mein, almost Hoovering a cold wonton, and sampling an egg fu yung pancake. Winnie chose the mu shu pork for herself and Richard wolfed down a little of this and a lot of that.

"Tea," I said between bites.

"I'll get it," Winnie said.

I held her back. "No, I will. I need to walk a little. Sugar all around?"

"Good for me," Richard said.

"Me, too," Winnie said.

"Anybody know where the kitchen is?"

"In the belly of the beast," Richard said in awful piratical parody.

I found it on the first floor and turned the switch for the overhead light. The copper kettle sat on the stove. I shook it and heard enough sloshing, so I lit the front burner with a long match and reached down the teapot and three mugs. I found the tea in the fourth cupboard I opened. Ordinary black tea would do. Now for a tray. I was searching the bottom cupboards when I came to one with cleaning supplies in it and caught a glimpse of a small, round container with a picture of a rat on it. I stared at it, wondering if this could possibly tie into the attempt on Vincent's life. Well, I had to do it or it would drive me crazy. So I pulled a couple of paper bags out of the pantry cupboard and gingerly dropped the container into it, double bagging the danged thing. Shivering with complete and utter terror, I pulled a bar of black soap from the windowsill and scrubbed my hands in a basin with some hot water from the kettle and a little cold water to make it just under scalding. By the time I finished, my hands were red and stinging. I was just about to use a cookie sheet for a tray when I saw a whole pile of trays on top of the cupboard near the door. When everything was ready, I clutched the bag in my left hand and balanced the tray with my right, leaning it against my hip.

Wow, Aggie, you haven't dropped anything yet! Good going.

The light switch was impossible, so I left it on, intending to shut it off after I cleaned up the tea things later. When I got to the stairs I contemplated the first obstacle. *Just take the first step carefully. Good. Now the second. Whoops! Hold it steady. One more step.* I looked up and counted. I got to ten before I noticed a pair of shoes, grey pants, a belt buckle, blue pin-striped shirt and blond mustache twitching above a silly grin.

"Need some help with that?"

"Of course I do."

Richard came down and took the tray from me. "What's that in your hand?"

"Rat poison."

"Joking, right?"

"Nope. Found it in the broom closet. Thought Winnie might

be able to tell us . . . oh, my God!"

"What?"

"I know what Donato was trying to tell me."

CHAPTER SIXTEEN

There they were, lined up like sentries: the accumulation of Donato's life. The photographs and paintings.

"Bring the tea upstairs, and then come down here and help me."

Before he went back upstairs, Richard saw that I was taking the photographs off the wall. "Of course! Donato pointed outside of the room. Aggie, you're a genius."

"We won't know that until we can figure out what's in these photos that ties into this mess."

"Something will be there. He used up all his energy so you would see it."

"We need someone who knows all about this, these people, the old country. Would Tiny know?"

"Come up right now and have some tea. I'll call Tiny. He'll drive like a maniac to get here."

I carried the photos in my arms up the stairs behind Richard. Winnie was still finishing up the Chinese food. A clock *bong*ed somewhere in the house and I realized that it was only seven o'clock. The kitchen had no window in it, so it had been dark; but the sun was only now beginning to set. Seagulls squawking outside alerted me to the beauty of the multicolored sky. Sailboats skidded over the waves, and fishermen whicked their rods hard to scale their lines way out into the channel. Such beauty in this world—and so much ugliness and hatred. Or was it greed? Vincent's organization made piles of money; I had seen one pile in the safe where my pretty little gun was being stored. How many more piles were there? Dozens? Hundreds? To some people, a hundred dollars was more than enough to attack someone to get. Hundreds of piles of money might seem worth killing to acquire.

I accepted the mug of tea that Richard prepared and sipped it slowly while he went to the phone and had the operator connect him with Tiny. After a short explanation, Richard yelped and held the phone away from his ear. Streams of angry words burst out of the earpiece.

I jumped up and snatched the phone out of Richard's hand. "Swear all you want in the car. Just get to Donato's retreat!" I replaced the handset in the receiver and went back to the sofa in the corner. "Do you think Vincent has had a chance to tell Tiny about his father?"

"I doubt it," Richard said. "Tiny acted like he was hearing about Donato's death for the first time."

"Oh, dear! I didn't want to be the one to tell him."

"We'll do it together."

Winnie drained her mug and began clearing up. "Meanwhile, I will wash up these things and change Donato's bed linens. There must be a parlor in this place. Why don't you two set up shop there and let me handle things up here?"

"The housekeeper can do that tomorrow."

"Let me, Aggie. I think best when I'm working."

"Okay, Richard, let's go find us a comfortable spot with a table. I want to study these photos while we wait for Tiny."

Downstairs, the boathouse still possessed the skeleton of what it had originally been. The wide open spaces surrounding the front entrance could have been used to store boats or repair them. Now its soft sofas and chairs served for entertaining. "It must have been remodeled recently, don't you think?"

"Yeah, maybe." Richard whipped open door after door

around the perimeter, all leading to storage closets. "Guess they had lots of tack or sails or whatever the heck they need for boats."

"A sail room! They must have had a sail room. There should be a table in there. If worse comes to worst, we'll use the floor."

The sail room was way in the back, behind the kitchen. The table was long, pine, with a golden hue that told of decades of use. We spread out the photos one by one, the same way they had been hung on the wall.

"Wasn't there a coat of arms?" Richard asked.

"Did you take it off the wall?"

"No. Did you?"

"Darn my socks! I didn't even notice that it was missing."

"He took it."

I didn't have to ask who *he* was. The ghost. The man-snake. The killer.

Frantically, I looked around the room. There were dozens of drawers, and I pulled open each one. "Here, paper, paper, paper." I slammed the last drawer hard. "Not a scrap. I want to re-create the goldarn shield."

"Vincent has a copy."

"No, he doesn't. His is different. But maybe I could just add the differences. The knife and the three fleur de lis."

"That's it. We'll get a copy of Vincent's and re-create Donato's."

"Why did he take it?"

Richard also didn't have to ask who *he* was. "Beats me."

"Someone else's story? That doesn't make much sense." I examined the spire in one of the photos. "Where did Donato come from?"

"Capodimonte?"

"You're not sure?"

"I always thought the restaurant was named after the town,

but maybe it wasn't. Maybe it just means what it means. You know—top of the mountain?"

"Capo means top?"

"Sort of, yes."

"I really need an Italian dictionary."

"It could also mean head."

"And here I thought it meant cap."

"It could mean that, too."

"And they say English is complicated!" I shook my head with frustration and scanned the first few photos, hoping to get some inspiration, some idea of what Donato had wanted me to see. Women, men, children, villages. No, one village. Different angles, but enough similarities in structures and decorations so that you could tell it was one village. I thought I saw something familiar and looked closer. "Well, imagine that. Richard, take a look. Do you see what I see?"

"It's just an old photo of a bunch of young thugs with plenty of fire power."

"That's the shadow on the wall. Look at the details. Look at their faces."

"Hey! This guy looks like Carlo."

"I think that's Donato."

"And the others?"

"The partners, maybe?"

"I don't see a Tiny there."

"That's because he's here and broke every record to do it," Tiny said. He stood in the doorway and surveyed the room. "Great setup. Give me something to do. I'm still reeling from the news of Donato's death." He held up a sack. "Thought we'd toast the old Don's life."

Richard and I looked at each other, each urging the other to step in and explain the real circumstances of Donato's death, neither of us wanting to be the one to do it.

"Perhaps this . . ." I waved at the photos. ". . . can wait until after the toast. I could use a drink." I linked my arm with Tiny's. "What did you bring?"

"I notice you and the other sister liked Asti, so I thought, why not?"

"Open the bottle, Tiny. I'll get glasses," Richard offered. "Aggie, you call Winnie. We can relax down here in the front parlor."

There were overstuffed chairs with ottomans, and Tiny commandeered one. When we all got settled, he lifted his glass. "To Donato, an original."

"Donato," we each said.

I couldn't tell him then. Not then. But I couldn't *not* tell him. It wouldn't have been fair. We might need his help. He might have some answers. He might not. But if we withheld the truth, it would be like stealing an important part of him—the right to know what had happened to his father. I knew that Vincent wanted to wait until after the funeral; but Tiny had been in on this from the beginning. To hold back now didn't make sense.

"Tiny?"

"Yes, Sister?"

"I . . . that is, *we* have something to tell you."

"Look," Richard said, "none of us wants to tell you this, but you have a right to know."

Richard had the floor. Richard had the lead. He and Tiny were friends. He knew best what to say. Unlike Carlo, Tiny went quiet when Richard was finished.

He finally said, "Let's get the animal who did this." He drained his glass of wine. "Show me what you found." He took one look at the photos and his eyes lit with professional glee. "Whooee. Victorian splendor, these prints. Really well done." He traced the face of one of the older men. "My grandfather. I have his formal portrait at home." When he got to the four

173

compatriots, he nodded. "There they all are. I take it this is Donato?" When Richard and I nodded, he said, "This handsome guy is my father. About the age he was when he emigrated here, I'd guess. And these must be Amadeo and Paolo, my father's cousins. We're the DiSilva branch, they're the Santini."

"And these other guys?" Richard asked, pointing to three other *banditti* photos.

"Got me. We'll need someone from the village to identify them."

"Aaargh!" Richard said. "We can't put an ad in the *Journal*. We can't ask mourners at the wake or we might alert the killer that we're hot on his trail."

"Well," Winnie said, "you could ask those people from the Hill, the ones we met this afternoon."

"Winnie, I shouldn't be so amazed," I said. "You're the best! There were two women. What were their names?"

"Well, one was Josephine something," Winnie said.

"Josephine Car something," Richard said.

I sat up straight, excited that I remembered anything about that afternoon. "It was Cardi. But she's not the important one. The woman we want to talk to is Mrs. Violetta Carcieri! My pupil's mother. I'm so tired, I forgot. She had a cigar box she was holding for Donato."

"He's not going to need it now," Tiny said. "Oh, man, he did love his cigars."

I frowned. Something was poking at my brain, but I couldn't put my finger on it. "That's what she said." It was something about the cigars or the ransom. *Which, Lord? I've been all alone here. You promised to stay close, so where are You? Vacation in the Alps? The catechism never mentioned a godly vacation. Hope You had a great time. Oh, thanks!* "That other woman—the one who told us about her cousin or nephew—her name was Bell something."

"Belson?"

"Winnie, dear, that's not an Italian name," Richard said.

"Well, it began with bell."

The Lord was finally in there pitching. *Thank You.* "Beltri. The mother is still alive. She prays for Donato."

"We need to see her and Josephine Carcieri first thing in the morning."

"Violetta's shop might be something like Carcieri's Smoke Shop. But we don't know anything about the Beltri family. We don't know where the mother lives. We don't have a telephone number. We don't even have a first name."

"But the cathedral has lists of everyone in the Diocese, including their origination. One call to the monsignor and we'll have the information in short order." Richard picked up the glasses. "I'm taking you and Winnie back to the convent, Aggie. Gather up the photos while I put these in the kitchen. Tomorrow is another day."

"I'd like to take the photo of my father," Tiny said. "Professional curiosity. Just want to know what they were printed on. Maybe I can make a reproduction, print a couple for the family. Is that okay with everybody?"

"Fine with me," I said.

"Sure, why not?"

"Richard, you're responsible to get the coat of arms from Vincent."

"Check."

"I'll call Monsignor Grace in the morning." I looked around at our small peace force. "We have three days to figure this out. If we don't, we won't be able to stop the killing."

CHAPTER SEVENTEEN

Sister Noble had kitchen duty again and let us in with a "Hush!" and a finger to her lips. I put my sack with a few of the photos in it next to the ice box and noticed that Sister Justina had fallen asleep at the table once more, her hand still around her evening's ration of milk. We would have tried to wake her, but several attempts at other times had led to naught, so it was best to let her be, but with a pillow under her head.

"Never mind hushing," I told Sister Noble. "A train could come through here and she wouldn't notice."

Winnie shouldered her sack and went to fetch a down pillow. When she came back, we settled the elderly nun's head in a more comfortable position, then took Sister Noble into the corridor leading to the back stairs.

"Don't let her lie on the bare table again," Winnie said. "She's our elder sister. She deserves our gratitude and our respect."

"I'm sorry, Sisters. It's the first time she fell asleep when I was on duty."

"You'll learn," I said, as if I had learned. But maybe I had. There were many things I was doing now that Mother Frances had taught me. Funny, but I suddenly realized that I missed her. She kept me on my toes—probably as much as I kept her on her toes. What would Winnie call that? Ah, yes. Symbiotic relationship. Probably that was very true.

"Monsignor Grace's assistant called," Sister Noble said. "He

176

says there's been no response from Ireland yet. What's in Ireland?"

"The Blarney Stone," Winnie said.

"Good night, Sister Noble."

"Good night, Sisters."

I stopped outside my cell and turned, pressing my back against the door frame. "I don't know if I can sleep tonight. There's so much that's changed and so many people counting on us. What if we can't do it, Winnie?"

"You'll do what you can, Aggie. There's no more that can be asked of you."

"I wish I hadn't given Richard my . . ."

"Don't you dare say it! If you want it back, you're going to have to get it approved by Mother Frances . . ."

"Ack! She'll kill me."

". . . or the Chancery."

"Not a chance."

"Oh, Aggie!"

I giggled. "Night, my friend."

I had refreshed myself and donned my shift before I remembered that my sack with the photos was still in the kitchen. Darn my socks! Where was my head? I pulled on my bathing robe and padded down the hall and the back stairs. I didn't turn on an electric light because I was used to moving around in the dark. But the *kitchen*—which was always lit in case someone needed food or help—shouldn't have been dark.

Now I really wished I had that gun! For a substitute, I grabbed an umbrella from the stand next to the telephone table and eased open the kitchen door. I reached for the electric light switch and turned it so the kitchen was bathed in light. "Bloody heck!" I reacted without thinking and rushed to Sister Noble's side. She was prone on the floor, a gash on the side of her head.

The back door was ajar, and my sack was gone.

"Blast! Blast! Blast! Blast! Blast!"

"Enough, Aggie! You've been saying that for the past twenty minutes. Even Josiah couldn't make you shut up."

"He took the sack. Those precious photos."

"He gave Sister Noble a great whack on the head, and she's not making this much of a fuss. Besides, we still have my sack, and there are more photos in it than there were in yours."

Josiah poked his head into the front parlor. "The doc finished bandaging her head. She should be okay, but she has to drink lots of coffee and stay awake. He said if she falls asleep and can't be woken up, she'll have to go to the hospital. So somebody has to be with her to keep her awake. And one of the beat cops found this a couple of yards down." He held up the sack and four frames, empty except for a few shards of glass in the corners.

"He didn't even leave the glass," Winnie said.

That was perplexing. "Why would he smash the glass, take the photos and leave the frames? Why not take the whole thing?"

Josiah gave me that *you-have-to-be-kidding* look, the one that used to get him a bloody nose from me when we were kids.

"Okay, what?" I asked him.

"He only wanted the contents."

"He could see the contents through the glass." Or could he? "Winnie, get the other photos."

When she got back to the kitchen, I was rummaging in the junk drawer to find a screwdriver. "What are you going to do, Aggie?"

I took one of the framed photos out of the sack. "Find out if there's anything underneath here that he might have been look-ing for." I gingerly bent back the nails that held the cardboard backing and pried it up and off. "Nothing between the two cardboards." I took up the last cardboard. "What's this?" The back of the photo was filled with writing. "Names and dates. Winnie, get some knives for you and Josiah and start prying."

Each photo had something on the back of it, but the ink was brown and slightly faded. Worse, the handwriting differed from photo to photo, none of them totally legible to me, and—blast it—all in Italian!

"We need Richard."

"We need sleep, Aggie, and so does he."

"I could take that down to the station for you," Josiah offered.

"No! Vincent would kill me."

"But we have a good strong safe and no one can get into it."

"Safe! *We* have a safe, too!"

"Where do we have a safe, Aggie? We don't have anything of value. Vows of poverty, remember?"

"But Father Lawton does. They keep the collection money in it. It's a big, old safe, too. Really strong."

Now Winnie was looking at me as if I was crazy. "Father Lawton and the new curate are fast asleep, and Mrs. Monaghan went home hours ago."

"That's what a night bell is for," I said.

"Night bells are for emergencies!"

"This *is* an emergency."

While we were arguing, Josiah had diligently been removing each of the photos from the frames. He knew me well, and must have figured that I'd win this argument as I'd won so many others over the years.

"Thanks, Josiah."

"No problem. Want me to run them over there? After all, this is police business."

Winnie and I looked at each other. "Yes!" we both said at once.

179

"I'll take my leave, then. Call if you need anything else."

"Are you going to find him, Josiah?"

"Not with the description your young nun gave. *It was dark,* she said. As mad as you used to make me, there was one thing I could count on—that you weren't a bubble-headed nincompoop. It was dark! Like saying it was night. Where do these brainless women come from?"

I held my tongue; but coming from him, whom the whole family thought would flunk out of police school . . . well, he and Sister Noble could have been bookends. Like Josiah, she wasn't the brightest bulb in the chandelier, but she was good-hearted, like Sister Justina. The order took what it could get and molded them into serviceable nuns. Justina, in household tasks, Noble, in . . . what were her skills? Not office work. Rosalia did that. Suddenly I realized that Mother Frances was grooming Sister Noble to take over for Justina. It was a noble work, and fit more than her name; but it made me sad to realize that Mother Frances knew too well that Justina would not be with us much longer. She was still there in the kitchen, sleeping comfortably, never knowing the house had been overturned by three policemen and a doctor, all of whom had quietly worked around her. I wondered how much time she had left, and quickly realized that if we didn't get this case solved within three days—no, two, now—none of us had much time left. The streets of Providence would go as the streets of Brooklyn, Chicago and Manhattan had gone. Bullets flying every which way made no safe place for anyone.

After we woke up Sister Brendan to keep Sister Noble awake and man the back door, I went to sleep thinking, "I really have to get an Italian dictionary."

Seven hours later, I woke up to the certainty of that dictionary's importance. Here was a case where knowing how to speak the language of our parishioners was imperative, and we two Irish nuns were fumbling in the dark because we didn't.

After six a.m. Mass, the sisters repaired to the kitchen to heat up the soup they had made the day before—beef, barley and lots of vegetables—from half the meat Vincent had sent over. Hearty enough for those who had nothing. Only Sister Noble had been excused. Winnie and I were in charge of distribution—which meant we had to hand the other sisters whatever they needed in the soup line.

"Put me to work," Richard said when he arrived.

"Nothing to do unless you want to help us with something else."

"What's the something else?"

"Fluency with Italian."

"And French," Winnie said.

I gave her a roll of my eyes. "What in the world would I ever need French for?"

"If you get a transfer to Woonsocket, you wouldn't ask that question."

She was right. The parishioners there spoke Canadian French. "Okay, we'll get two dictionaries and after this case is over, Richard will teach us."

"I don't know French."

"So you'll teach us Italian. Lisette LaMalfa, the mother of one of my students, is from Montreal. Maybe we can rope her in to help us."

"Good plan," Richard said, "but could we please just stick to one problem at a time?"

"Darn my socks! I forgot to get the photos from Father Lawton."

"I'll put on a pot of coffee and then run over to the rectory." He spooned coffee into the basket and filled the new percolator with cold water. "Keep your eye on the pot, please, Winnie. Don't let it boil over. And don't let Aggie near it."

"I can make coffee!"

"The last time you made coffee, I chewed it."

"That was the first time. I've learned since then."

"Yep," Winnie said. "Now it's either dishwater or you need a cup of sugar and a quart of milk to make it palatable."

I turned around to argue my case with Richard, only to find that he had sneaked out during Winnie's and my bickering—or should I say bantering? Because, really, in the past three months I *had* learned how to make coffee. She and Richard were just so used to teasing me that they now did it automatically. And I accepted it automatically, too, even though my skills as cook and keeper of the flame had changed. One more thing for which I could thank Mother Frances. Maybe if she had had enough time, she could have nudged me into the right notes at Catherine's Mass. My goodness, was that only four days ago? Yes. This was Friday, the fifth day. The Good Lord created the whole world in only seven. Hopefully, we could stop our tiny part of the world from being destroyed in three.

Richard came back with the photos. "Hey, these are interesting. There's a whole lot of information about Donato and his cronies."

He showed us one of the prints. "This is Donato with his sister."

"He had a sister?"

"Apparently. But . . ." He flipped the print over. "It says here *scomparsa*—that's disappearance or disappeared—and the date of June 19, 1885."

"Disappeared? How does somebody disappear?"

"Well, it's not a miraculous event, Aggie. Lots of girls disappear into, uh . . ."

"Prostitution."

"Yeah."

"Do you think that's what happened?"

"I don't know. There are four other young girls who went *scomparsa*. But according to two photos, so did two old men and four young bucks. So I think something else was going on in those hills."

The soup line broke up and Richard put the photos in Mother Frances' office, where no one would disturb them. We all helped the rest of the nuns clean up. Richard sidled up to me and whispered, "Why aren't they talking?"

"Clean first, talk later."

"Mother Frances?"

I nodded. "It works."

We were finished in record time, mostly because Richard pitched in and scoured the huge soup pots. The nuns thanked him profusely for the wedding cookies, fixed tea and retired to the large dining room to drink their favorite beverage, eat the leftover cookies and do a little maintenance sewing. Even without Mother Frances, the daily schedule was still in effect, a further testament to her strong influence. I was beginning to appreciate the little things she did, and acknowledge the huge impact she had in making all our lives more orderly and serene.

What was waiting at the front door when the bell rang was hardly serene, however. Tiny swooped in, waving a folder in the air.

"This," he said, "will blow everything wide open. And it can't end any way but bad."

CHAPTER EIGHTEEN

"What could be that incendiary?" Richard asked.

"A will. At least, it almost sounds like a will." I pushed Tiny and pulled Richard into the back parlor usually reserved for us nuns. Standing close together, we passed the document from one to the other.

"The wording is strange," Richard said.

"Tell me about it," Tiny said.

"It's in Italian, Richard!"

"Have patience, Aggie. We'll figure it out. *Tontino.* What's a tontine?"

Holy cow! "I know."

Eye rolls from Winnie and Richard. "You don't know Italian, remember?"

"Ah, but we studied this in our castles and knights lesson. See, some Italian or Swiss or French guy made up this investment scheme, where each person put the same amount of money into a pot and the last man living gets it all. Is it about money?"

"Sort of," Tiny said. "A coin with two heads."

"That's all?"

"No." Tiny squinted at the faded ink and read the contents in a short list. "A knife, a black flannel cap, and the foot of a chicken."

"I know what that is, too!" More eye rolls. "Well, I do! It's the family crest. The one that was on the wall at the boathouse.

The one that has a few things different from Vincent's version—like a knife, which isn't there in Vincent's version, a chicken that looks a lot like a Rhode Island Red and not the brown one on the invitation, and only three fleur de lis, where Vincent's had a whole slew of them."

The room got really quiet. Richard and Tiny kept sneaking glances at each other, and even Winnie had a problem landing her gaze on something.

"I give in!" Richard said. "What the hell does all this mean?"

"Richard, you are in a convent. Watch your language!"

"Sorry, Aggie, but none of this makes sense."

"Of course it does."

Tiny took the largest chair in the room. "I'm all ears. Enlighten me."

Ears? He was long legs, too, stretched out onto the worn Turkey rug. All man, but a nice specimen. Richard and Winnie chose the sofa, while I shut the door. I hesitated, wanting to take Mother Frances' chair, but opting for the small slipper chair where Sister Justina usually sat. I could not see myself in Mother Frances' chair. It was hers. To me, it would always be hers.

When I was finally settled, I collected my thoughts before plunging into this all-important lesson. "What you have to understand is that a coat of arms started out as an heraldic design for every major house. At first, coats of arms were very simple. One color per family or house. Like the House of Stuart, which was blue, or the House of Orange, which was, well, orange, of course. Kings had their favorite color and usually had their personal animal—lion or hawk or deer—embroidered on the field color. A son of the King could use the lion, but he had to make the distinction between his father and himself, so the bar system came into effect. Hence, they divided the banner. The son's choice of animal went on top and his father's

185

shifted to below the bar. Is that clear?"

"Got it," Richard said. Tiny merely nodded, and Winnie looked bored.

"Okay, I'll speed it up."

"Thanks be to God," Winnie said.

"Over the years, this war banner became an identifying mark or crest or coat of arms for each family, and it became more complicated as the family changed. The animals were replaced by something special to the family—like an open Bible for a cleric or a transom or triangle for an architect. The shield for the Society of Masons is one of those kinds of coats of arms. We even have that one on the dollar bill. The eye and the triangle are old heraldic symbols. Anybody want a cup of coffee?"

All three said, "Yes!"

Five minutes later, I sat with a mug of Vincent's really good coffee and a pad of paper.

"Okay, watch."

I sketched the outline of the coat of arms, knowing full well that I was no artist. But a sketch needed only to suggest.

"The cap in Donato's coat of arms is centered here at the top, meaning it's the most important part of the shield. The knife lies on its side beneath the cap, meaning that it has some kind of relationship with the cap, and a very important one or it would be under the horizontal bar, which in this case comes right underneath the knife. From that horizontal bar is a vertical one, set right in the middle, leading from the horizontal bar to the bottom of the crest. The chicken is on the left which usually relates to the paternal side of the family. The three fleur de lis are on the right, which usually relates to the maternal side of the family."

"Clear as this coffee," Winnie said.

Now I was miffed. "Hey!"

"I take it black, remember?"

"To continue, class!"

Winnie groaned, but Tiny leaned over and pointed to the not-quite-round shape at the top. "Cap. Capo."

A light bulb went off over or inside Richard's head. "Capo. Head."

"Or leader, like Donato," Tiny said. "But why the knife and all the rest of this stuff? They don't have anything to do with him. And what about the list in this tontine thing? How do they relate with this?"

"Ahem!"

"You want to explain, I suppose, Aggie?"

"Yes, Winnie, I do. Of course, this is only an educated guess, but I think it will hold together." I pointed to the list. "I can figure out that the cap on the list is this cap. The knife is this knife. And the foot of the chicken must be the foot of the original chicken. See, all of these things are symbols. They stand for something important in the history of the family. I emphasize family—but that doesn't necessarily mean biological family. For the Masons, it's the Society of Masons. Tiny, does it say what kind of knife we're dealing with?"

"Coltello di marcellaio."

Richard looked astonished. "Knife of the butcher? What's a butcher got to do with Donato's family? He was just a farmer in Italy."

"Was he? I don't see a single farm in these photos. There are small houses, a church in the background, buildings and mountains, but no gardens or vineyards or orchards or animals other than a couple of donkeys and horses. If he was a farmer, wouldn't he want to show off his labors?"

Richard and Tiny flipped through the photos, tossing each into a pile in the middle of the table. "Fu—"

"Richard!"

"For crying out loud, how do you see what we can't?"

Winnie groaned and buried her head in her hands. "Oh, no. Here comes Plato and that ding-dong allegory."

"I'll spare you."

"Thank God."

"I look carefully and then try to connect the dots. In this case the dots are the coat of arms and the will. Richard, you asked what the butcher's knife had to do with Donato. I think the answer to that will lead us to the killer. He wanted the coat of arms. He wanted the photos. He obviously also wanted the will. They're so important to him that he was willing to kill the three partners, Catherine, even Donato himself—in fact, every single person in the hierarchy of Donato's *family*—to get them."

"There's something else in this will-thing that I didn't understand," Tiny said. Three heads swiveled and waited expectantly. *"Scatola di sigaro."*

Richard furrowed his brow. "Cigar box?"

"Si. Uh, yes. The things on this list are to be found in a cigar box."

Winnie whooped. "I know this one!"

We both stared down the gentlemen's incredulous looks. "She really does," I said.

Winnie very nearly preened. "The Carcieri's cigar shop. Yesterday Mrs. Carcieri told us that they've been holding a cigar box for Donato for years. From time to time, he and his partners used to go there to see the box. I'll bet inside it you'll find the cap, the knife and the foot of the chicken."

"The money, too, maybe," I said. "The two-headed coin. All four of those things—the symbols of the family, the business family in this case—to be inherited by the last man standing. That's what this tontine is all about."

Tiny's chair tilted backward when he jumped up, but Winnie caught it and pulled it out of the way so it wouldn't crash onto the floor and scare the other sisters out of a year's growth.

"Wait a minute! Are you saying that the person who has those symbols gets control of the family and the businesses?"

"I don't know. I can't read Italian. Is that what the will says?"

Richard read the will shoulder to shoulder with Tiny. I held my breath, hoping that it was not going to be as easy as that. If those symbols, those things in the cigar box, were going to be used to change the makeup of the Donato organization, then all hell would break loose. *Sorry, Lord, but You know it's true. The Devil will have his due, and it won't be healthy for anyone.*

Tiny finished reading the will a tad before Richard. "There's not a word in here about inheritance of the organization. Just inheritance of the things on the list."

Winnie said, "Maybe we better go get the things on the list! Surely Mrs. Carcieri will give the cigar box to you, Aggie."

"With a little help from someone we all know at the Chancery, maybe." I turned to Tiny. "Do you know where the cigar store is?"

"On the Hill, where else?"

"Let's go," Winnie insisted. "Maybe we can get another one of those shorties. Or pizza. I'm really getting to like that neighborhood."

"We can't fit into that tin can of yours, Richard, so we'll take my car," Tiny offered.

"I'll be right with you," I said. "I'll just make a short call to the Chancery and tell the other sisters that we're going out."

They were waiting patiently when I came out to the curb. "No word yet from Ireland. Monsignor Grace has an important meeting with Bishop Keough which could go on all day, but he'll call Mr. Carcieri as soon as he can to tell him about Donato's death and urge him to give us the box."

The parking situation was a repeat of the day before. Tony had another of those softcover books, a colorful picture of a cowboy on a horse on the cover. "Tom Mix?"

"You know it! Very exciting."

Probably not as exciting as getting shot at and chasing down the murderer of six people. How did I get myself into these things? No wonder Mother Frances despairs.

We stopped for shorties all around, and Richard did his quarter trick again. As I munched on the sausage and peppers, I noticed that many of the shops had photos of Donato in their windows and black crepe and bunting strung from side to side. "Look at that! You'd think the Holy Father had died."

"Donato was closer to these people than the Holy Father," Tiny said. "So was my father. They hung crepe for him, too. I remember that the day after his death Don Ricci was here, walking these streets and alleyways, listening to people's woes and trying to fix them. Most of the time, he did."

The cigar store was at the junction of two short streets. A pizza parlor on one corner, a cleansers on another, and a flower shop on the third. A bell tinkled when we opened the door, and the strong aroma of imported Italian cigars gave a bite to the air.

Violetta Carcieri met us with open arms. "Oh, Sister, we were devastated to hear last night of Don Ricci's death. It was such a shock, and here we were, the four of us, talking of him only yesterday." She shook hands with Richard and Tiny, who introduced themselves. "Monsignor Grace just called. My husband Salvatore isn't here at the moment. He had some business on the other side of the city, but I'm sure he'd want to accommodate the Chancery." She motioned us to follow her into the back, which was separated from the front salesroom by a bright red curtain. "We don't keep anything in the safe anymore. Just Don Ricci's box." She twirled the dial on the safe and lined up the arrow on spots whose numbers were long worn off. How did she know where to stop? Probably by years of use, the way I could get dressed in the dark, even pinning on my veil and cowl with straight pins and no mirror. There was an audible *click* and the door popped open. Reaching inside, she brought out a dented and very dusty cigar box with a paper label of a black lily on the top. "Here we are. I'll just dust it off."

"You don't have to do that," I said. "We'll take it as it is."

"Will you display it at the wake?"

"I don't know. Vincent will make that decision."

"Well, it's probably best to have it back in the family where it belongs." She hefted it. "Funny, but it's not moving."

"Mrs. Carcieri, the box can't move on its own."

"No, not the box. The contents. They usually slide back and forth when I lift it." She shook it gently. "Oh, dear!" Her complexion—pink and healthy a moment before—now drained of all color and she staggered, thrusting the box at me. "I promise I didn't do anything. It's been locked away all these years except when Don Ricci and the others came to see it."

I lifted the lid and peered inside. "Is there no end to the Devil's work?"

The cigar box was completely empty.

CHAPTER NINETEEN

"He's been here."

Nothing could induce me to look at Tiny. He had lost a father before he should have. Nor at Richard, who had been taken in by Donato and given a home. Nor at Mrs. Carcieri, who gave signs that she was a wreck over something she couldn't control. Did she think she was going to be punished by these men for losing the contents of the box?

How had she lost the contents of the box?

Wait! How had she known about Donato's death?

I went to her where she had slipped to the floor, and took her trembling hands in mine. "Mrs. Carcieri, did you say you heard last night that Donato had died?"

"Yes," she whispered. "*Dio mio!* How did this happen? How did we lose the things in the box?"

"Who told you about Donato's death?"

Tiny leaned over. "Good Lord, she knew before Vincent released the announcement?"

"That's what I'm trying to find out. Mrs. Carcieri, who told you?"

"*Mio sposo.*"

"What do you mean, your husband?"

Oh, dear Lord, calm Tiny down. He's getting all red in the face and he's going to scare this poor woman half to death.

I tried to keep my voice calm and gentle. "Mrs. Carcieri, who told your husband?"

"I don't know. I was upstairs making supper when the bell over the door rang. Salvatore went to see who it was. He came back so upset. After he told me that the Don was dead, we turned off the stove, put Donato's photo in the window and draped the bunting right away."

"Where did you say your husband is?"

"I don't know where he is. He said he had important business on the East Side and would be back for lunch."

"When do you usually eat lunch?"

"Noon."

I looked at the big clock on the wall. It was nearly one o'clock. "Is he ever this late?"

She started to cry. "Never before."

The bell over the door sounded. Her head came up. "Salvatore!" She leaped to her feet. "Salvatore! Sister Agnes is here." She pulled open the red curtain and stopped. "No."

The blue uniform was enough for me, and apparently Mrs. Carcieri, to know what had happened. The official expression on the young cop's face put a period to my thoughts.

"Get her a chair, Tiny," I whispered. "Richard, we'll need some whiskey or wine. Find it. Winnie . . ."

"I'm here. I know."

The officer began with the usual. "Mrs. Carcieri, I'm sorry to inform you . . ."

That was as far as he got before she screamed and went limp. Winnie and I caught her, holding her up until Tiny put a chair behind her knees so she could slump into the chair and not end up on the floor again. I thought Irish mothers and wives had the market sewn up on keening mourners. I was wrong. Italians—with their foreign phrases—made it an art. Sounds interspersed with prayers. Prayers with what must have been invectives, it was so punctuated with venom and fear both. I knew what *figlio de putana* meant but was pretty sure that was the mildest of the swearing she did. The other words were accompanied by spitting and the universal symbol of devil horns.

How right she was. But the police, at whom she cursed, were not the culprits. Salvatore was dead, like all the others.

I pulled the young officer outside. "He was murdered?"

"Yes."

"How?"

"Knifed."

Oh, dear Lord! What if it was with that knife that had been rattling around in the cigar box? How ironic if he had saved the weapon that killed him. *Yes, Lord, I know that Satan is alive and well and waits for occasions like this. And, yes, we will all be on our guard.* "I'd like you to do something for me," I told the police officer.

"She has to identify the body."

"I know, but I need to talk to my cousin, Sergeant Morgan."

"Josiah Morgan?"

"That's the one. Do you know if he's on duty? He was working last night."

"No, ma'am. It's his morning off."

"Then I can call him myself." I smiled at him. "It must be dreadful to have to bring this kind of news to people. I'm sorry you have to do it, but I'm grateful to you that you didn't make it worse than it is. Don't worry, I'll see to it that Mrs. Carcieri gets to the morgue."

"Thank you, ma'am."

Ma'am. He wasn't Catholic, and I felt a hundred years old.

Because we had to see one more person, but mostly because the order's rules didn't allow companions to split up, it was going to be Winnie's and my responsibility to get information from Mrs. Beltri on our own. It was best for Tiny and Richard to take Mrs. Carcieri to view her husband's remains. She was going to need propping up, and they were strong enough to do it.

The two of them—pigheaded men that they were—didn't agree that we should visit the Beltris on our own.

"Richard can go with you," Tiny said. "I can handle one hysterical woman."

Thanks to more help from Monsignor Grace, it took us only twenty minutes to find the right Beltri family. They lived in a third-floor tenement which showed the care they had put into it, but also the straitened circumstances they were in. They weren't homeless, but they were teetering on the edge and could fall over if this Depression got worse, of that I was certain.

In the midst of faded curtains and threadbare carpets sat the tiniest, frailest woman I had ever seen. Emilia Beltri, however, sat straight, even though her feet didn't touch the floor. She had a broad smile that showed more gum than teeth, but it lit the room—until we told her what we were there for. In a blink, her clear brown eyes clouded over and a terrible sadness seemed to pull her body in on itself. She spoke in Italian, but luckily Richard was with us so he could translate.

"I don't like to think of those times," she said. "It was fifty years ago."

Her daughter Rita pulled me aside. "She had nightmares when we were little. She's better now. Do you have to bring this up?"

"If we want to catch Don Ricci's killer, yes, we do."

"*Dio mio!* He was murdered?"

"Yes. The police are investigating, but they don't know who did it. From what you told me yesterday, I think his murder might be tied into the troubles they had in their village a long time ago. She's the only one who knows what happened. If we have any hope of finding this killer, we need her information now."

"Okay." She went to her mother. "Mama, just tell them one thing. That's all they need. One thing."

Richard translated her words: "Rita, you want me to live through that again?"

"I'm here, Mama. And it's not that time anymore. We're in America, Mama. You're always protected here, aren't you?"

The word America must have sparked something in Mrs. Beltri, because she struggled to speak in English. "*Si*. Don Ricci, he here, *suora*."

"That means nun," Richard said.

I looked up at Rita. "Tell her she can speak in Italian if it's easier. Richard can tell us what she's saying."

As the story unfolded, Winnie had to leave the room, she was so overcome. Towards the end, it was even difficult for Richard to voice in English the horror Mrs. Beltri had undergone at the hands of a man she alternately called *Don Ramo* and *Le Don Marcellaio*, the Butcher. She described what he did with a boning knife, how he ruled their little patch of earth with bestiality and butchery. Until Donato and his friends took it all away from him. She was exhausted when she finished, and her tears melted my heart until I ached for what she had gone through.

Rita slowly rose from her chair and trudged into the corner where the kitchen was. She turned on the tap and dashed water into her face. I went to her side and found her crying quietly. "My God, Sister. I didn't know about all that. I didn't know."

"Take good care of her. She's done something today that will bring justice and help us find Donato's killer. But there's one thing . . ."

"Yes, Sister?"

"Stay inside today."

"I need to go to market."

"I'll have a dinner delivered to you. But stay inside. We don't want to tip off the killer that we know about him. Tomorrow, I'll have a town car pick you up at seven to take you to the wake in style. Promise me, now."

"Of course. Anything. But . . ."

"Yes?"

"My mother, she doesn't eat cheese or drink milk. Bad stomach."

"Don't worry. The chef will prepare something wonderful without milk or cheese."

We thanked them profusely and walked back to Vincent's restaurant, where we were to meet up with Tiny. Not a word did we speak the whole nine blocks. This time, we went in the front door of Capodimonte Ristorante, and Richard escorted us to a small private dining room in the back behind the bar. A waiter appeared to take our order.

"I don't care," Winnie said.

I just shook my head.

"We're expecting Tiny soon, but just bring the shrimp special and an antipasto. Coffee now."

"Make mine tea, please," Winnie said.

"I need a good strong wine," I said. "Chianti."

"We'll need a whole teapot, black tea," Richard said. He reached into his pocket and pulled out a small package. "Forgot to give it to you before, but that awkward translation for Mrs. Beltri reminded me of it." He pushed it across the table to me.

"An English-Italian dictionary! Thank you, Richard. Of course I could have used it thirty minutes ago."

"You would have been flipping through pages and not keeping up, and it would have unnerved that poor, brave woman."

I put the dictionary in my pocket. "I told Rita we'd send them dinner tonight, and maybe we should include something for tomorrow's lunch, too."

"I'll take care of it."

"But we have to do more," I insisted. "They're living in a

nice place, but they have nothing. Mrs. Beltri's slippers were threadbare, and the stuffing was spilling out of the furniture." I thought for a moment, then got a great idea. *Or maybe it was from You, Lord, as are most good thoughts. I feel Your presence. Just keep me on the right track, please. And thank You.* "Richard, Montagne's, the Ricci's furnishings emporium. We have to send the designers in there and totally redo their tenement. And we have to assure them that they won't starve. So, since Vincent owns three restaurants, send them three good meals a week, and make sure there's enough for at least two meals in one."

Winnie leaned over and covered my hand with hers. "Oh, Aggie! That's splendid."

"Well, yes, that's easy," Richard said. "But what do we do with the information she gave us? How do we tie that in with the killings here? And how do we stop this madman from killing again?"

"We expose him," I said. "I'd like to do it at the wake when everyone who is anyone is there."

"Expose him? We don't even know who he is."

"What do you mean, we?"

"You know, Aggie?"

"I think so. I'm just not sure who the accomplice is."

CHAPTER TWENTY

You really could have knocked Richard over with a feather. He stared at me, totally flummoxed. "How do you know?"

"You know as much as I do. I'm surprised you don't see it."

"Oh, save us! It's Plato again."

"No, it isn't, Winnie. It's just common sense and your math progressions. Or is that permutations, or combinations? Anyway, it's when things begin to fit together, the answers just seem to come to me. Like a jigsaw puzzle. You have to turn each piece, examining the sides for all the bumps that might fit and trying until you find the one that does."

Winnie's forehead unfurrowed. "You mean like: *If you only had black socks and white socks and the lights went out in the house, how many socks would you have to pull out of your drawer to be certain you had a pair that matched?*"

"Close enough."

"What's the answer?"

"Richard! You're smarter than that!"

"My head's swimming with butchery. I don't have time for socks."

"Three. No matter what you pull out first and second, the third one will match one of them. I just weeded out all the extraneous things and what I was left with was one man, one very unbalanced man, who would do anything to get and keep his power. He may have started out a real butcher, but he ended up as the most hated and feared man in his part of the world.

And then he did one final thing to rile Donato and his friends. Remember, Donato's sister and Tiny's cousin are listed among the missing. After that, it was curtains."

"That doesn't tell me who did all this here."

"No. But we know it has to be someone in the family. Someone who can impersonate Vincent—or at least have people believe he speaks for Vincent. He has to be able to get close to Donato and the other partners, and have them let down their guard so much that they end up dead. Let's face it, there aren't many people who fit that description. So I lined them up like socks in the dark or jigsaw puzzle pieces in a pile. How many can you think of who can get that close?"

"You're not counting Tiny?"

"I didn't leave anyone out of my pile, including Tiny *and* Carlo."

"What?"

"Power. Vincent has it. His brother might want it."

"He wouldn't kill Catherine."

"No? Men have killed for much less."

"You didn't used to be this hard, Aggie."

"I'm not hard, Richard. I've just come to grips with the realities of the world we live in. Above everyone, you should know what that's like." The waiter returned with tea and coffee and a large platter of antipasto. "Send some food to the Beltri women, please. No milk. No cheese."

Richard left to give the order and directions to the men in the kitchen. Winnie poured the tea, and I took great care in sugaring and creaming my coffee. I took a sip and my gaze met Winnie's.

"Don't look at me like that, Win. You don't need to feel sorry for me. I know I get caught in the muck and I don't like it any better than you do, but it comes easily to me to figure out mysteries. Perhaps God wants me to do this, else why did He make it so easy for me to see what others don't?" I got up, put my arm around my friend's shoulder and hugged her. "I love you, dear friend. Everything is going to be okay as long as I know the difference between what's real and what isn't." I patted her pink cheek. "God and you and the convent are real. I have to call Josiah. Be right back."

I ran into Tiny in the alcove near the kitchen. Literally ran right into him.

"I heard what you said to Richard. You really suspected me?"

"I had to suspect everyone."

"Had to?"

"You wouldn't have been in on all this if you were still a suspect."

"When did I get eliminated?"

I giggled. "What egos men have! If you must know, you were on my pile for about, oh, five seconds."

"That long?"

We laughed easily with each other. "You're a really nice man. Now point me to somewhere private so I can call my cousin."

When I returned to the table, there were three pieces of lettuce and not much else on the antipasto plate. "Where's mine?"

"I ordered you a cold lobster cocktail," Tiny said.

"Yum." The lobster was all claws, the sweetest part, and the sauce was just spicy enough. "Double yum. I'm not sharing."

"What's his name?" Tiny asked.

Carefully, I put down my seafood fork and wiped my mouth. "Was this a bribe?"

"We need to know, Aggie," Richard said.

"Vincent needs to know. He made a promise. Are the two of you going to make the same promise?" When they didn't say anything, I pushed the rest of the lobster away. "I think Winnie and I will be taking a cab back to the convent." I stood up. "Now."

"Sit down, Aggie, please," Richard said. "I promise to do whatever Vincent promised to do."

"Hold off the war until Monday. Don't take the law into your own hands. Let me work it out."

Tiny bowed his head and his mouth worked as if he wanted to say something; but in a matter of moments, he looked at me and nodded. "You can't shoulder this alone. You'll need our help, and to get this madman I'll agree to everything Vincent agreed to. I think he already spoke for all of us, anyway."

"He might be able to speak for you in business, but this is personal more than business. Your father was murdered by this madman. I wouldn't expect you to forget that, but I hope you can settle for justice, not revenge. In any case, you're your own man and I respect your right to make your own decisions. That's all."

Tiny jumped up and pushed my chair against my legs. "Will you join us, Sister Agnes?"

"Thank you most kindly."

I took two more bites of lobster, chewing slowly.

"Oh, for crying out loud," Richard said, "who is he?"

I left the table and locked the door, then returned to the table and sipped on my wine for courage. "This is only between us four. No one else until I tie up all the loose ends." They nodded and I took a deep breath, letting out the name of someone who had destroyed a good mother, fathers who were loved if not good, and a young girl who might have been better than she was if given the chance. When I told them, the stunned looks on all three faces were exactly what I expected. "It all fits. While I was in the office calling Josiah, I looked in the Italian side of the dictionary you gave me, Richard. I needed to look up that word Mrs. Beltri kept using. *Ramo.* You translated it once or twice; but she said it over and over and over. So, it must have meant something important to her. And the way she said it, it seemed like she was spitting or swearing. What could be so powerful that it would cause such a lovely woman to turn an ordinary word into something vile? So I looked it up and . . . well, you know what I found."

"Could it be that simple?" Tiny asked. "He's jealous and wants more than he has?"

"It's not simple at all," I said. "Remember the will, the coat of arms and the years that have gone by. Fifty years. And now, when all the men who were involved in that horror in Italy are old and getting ready to die, he strikes? Does that signal greed to you, or something more, something, well, Italian?"

Tiny voiced it, but, really, it had been voiced first by Vincent. "Vendetta."

"Yes. When Vincent said *vendetta* to his dead father, it made me realize what was really going on. The killer could have struck at any time. Why now? Why not forty or thirty or twenty years ago?"

The doorknob turned a couple of times, then a knock sounded. "Let's leave it for now," I said. Richard got up to let the waiter in. The scent of shrimp and wine and garlic was so wonderful I wanted to cry. The first bite danced on my taste buds. "Oh, bliss! My first meal in heaven has to be shrimp scampi."

"What do we do now?" Richard asked.

"We prepare our case so we can present it at the wake."

"Why the wake?"

"Because everyone he's ever hurt will be there. Josiah and his forces will be there. Mrs. Beltri will be there. And she deserves to see him cut down. Also, his accomplice will be there. Of course I have to figure out who that is."

"You don't know?" Winnie asked.

"Not yet. I have my suspicions, but we'll have to go to the Chancery to see if there are any records to confirm them."

"Are you sure there's an accomplice?"

"Did I fail to mention that those seventeen bullet holes came from bullets shot from both the driver's side and the passenger's side? Oh, make no mistake. There's an accomplice. At least one, maybe more."

"Do you want dessert, or should we get going and then have dessert after?"

"After," Tiny said.

I nodded, but noticed that Winnie's mouth had decidedly downturned corners. "I'll call Father David, Monsignor Grace's assistant, and ask that coffee and a dessert tray be prepared."

"Sounds good," Tiny said.

The coffee was strong, and the lemon squares were plentiful. Winnie had three. I admit, I had more than one.

Father David carried in several parish record books. We took one look and knew we were in trouble.

"They're not listed by towns of origin," Richard said.

Tiny pounded the table, and I worried that he might lose his temper for real. "How will we be able to do this?" he asked no one in particular. "Damn!"

I put my hand on his shoulder. "There is one way. I think I know what we're looking for. At least, I have this feeling that the accomplice is one of two people. So we'll just look at those two. If one clicks, we have it—or them, if they both match."

I told Father David what we wanted to see and he helped us look. I worked with Tiny on one book. Richard and Winnie worked on another. It was Father David who found one of the names first. It matched.

Tiny traced the bold, black letters. "Holy Mother of God! How did this happen?"

"I'll explain it later. We have two more names."

"You mean one more."

"No, I mean two."

The first part of the ride to the convent was punctuated by Winnie's clacking rosary and Tiny's stifled exclamations of disbelief. The second part clarified what had happened and why.

"Of course, I'm only guessing," I said. "We'll find out if it's true from the reaction at the wake. Meanwhile, I'd like to find out if the cyanide in the container I found at the boathouse is the one that was used on the sugar cubes. Is there any way we can determine that, Winnie?"

"Possibly. It depends on the impurities. Carlo and I could work on separating them out. I can't guarantee it, but we can try."

"First thing in the morning. Tiny, can you get hold of Carlo and ask him to be at the convent at seven-thirty?"

"Done." He grabbed my hand as I was getting out. "Thank you, Sister."

"That's Aggie, Tiny."

Richard leaned over and chucked him under the chin. "Only family calls her that. Welcome to the family."

"I didn't know you were part of her family, DelVecchio," Tiny said to me.

"There are all kinds of family."

"Don't we know it."

Tiny's sedan was pulling away from the curb when I realized I needed something from Richard. I smacked the spare tire in the back and Tiny pulled to a stop and rolled down the window.

"Got a mate to that little gem you gave me, Richard?"

"You think you're going to need it?"

"I think somebody has to be ready just in case, and I can't see that Vincent is going to allow anyone in without being searched. With some exceptions, and I'm one of those exceptions."

"So are they," Tiny pointed out.

"So we have to have . . . what is it they call it . . . an ace in the hole?"

That night, as Winnie and I sat in our curtained-off private bathtubs, covered from neck to toe in a bathing dress, Winnie asked, "Aggie, do you know what you're doing?"

"Trying to keep this city from dying at the hands of a monster."

CHAPTER TWENTY-ONE

DeLuca's was the largest funeral home in Rhode Island that offered Italians the kind of service they were used to. It had one parking lot behind the converted mansion and two others that were used for overflow cars. That night, all three lots were filled, and both sides of the street were jammed with cars and trucks. On the porch just beside the entrance were burly men who pulled anyone aside they thought was suspect: man or woman. Some they patted down. Others were escorted to an alcove where they were subjected to a more intense search. Inside, other men with conspicuous bulges under their jackets and police out of uniform held strategic positions so they could see every spot in the room. A half dozen men even stood on tables to get a good line of vision.

When Winnie and I had arrived at six-thirty that evening, the viewing room was empty and we had time to say a prayer and give our sympathies to the family. Now, you could hardly breathe because of the crush of the crowd. The chairs that would have ordinarily been set up so everyone who wished could sit for a while and visit had been relegated to a storeroom in the basement. Only a few chairs and one sofa were set up for designated family and friends. Winnie and I led Mrs. Beltri and her daughter to two of those chairs, then sat beside them as a line of mourners snaked around the dimly lit room. Someone in a back room somewhere played operatic arias, church hymns and familiar Italian songs on a piano.

In the main viewing room, people streamed by Donato's casket in twos and threes. Vincent and Carlo both stood beside their father's coffin to welcome each of the mourners, say a few words, shake a hand, give a nod, and pass them along so the line kept moving.

Dante's Aunt Rachel spoke to each woman, distributing commemorative cards with a print of St. Anthony on the front and the Lord's Prayer on the back with Donato's name, birth and death dates. From personal experience, I knew that some of these cards would go into the family Bible or prayer book, while others would be used as ordinary bookmarks or thrown away within a week.

The world went on, and it would go on without Donato. But for this night and the next, the city held its breath and paid its respect.

"Is he here, Aggie?" Winnie asked. I inclined my head in the direction of the casket. "How much longer?"

"That's up to Josiah."

"Oh, look! There's Anna and Ella. They look so tired after all that's happened." Winnie followed the progression of the mourners. "So many people. Even some of his staff from the boathouse."

"And Dr. McMahon."

"Really?"

"If you don't have a backup, you don't have a plan."

"Dr. McMahon is your backup?"

"Part of it."

"Does anyone know everything you do?"

"Everyone who needs to know, knows some of it."

It was interesting to me, the diversity of the people who were attending this Saturday wake. Politicians and priests. Street women and nuns. Working people and business owners. Teachers and tramps. Donato had affected them all, one way or another.

Monsignor Grace came in quietly, approaching Vincent and Carlo with no trouble as the Catholics—who probably dominated those attending—gave way to a noted cleric. He said a word to Vincent and Carlo, turned to the casket, knelt on the reserved kneeler, and raised his hand in a blessing. The room quieted down quickly.

"In nomine Patris . . ." he began. *In the name of the Father.* Some of the faithful dropped to their knees and dug out their rosaries from pocket or purse. The sorrowful mysteries came next, and for twenty minutes the room and the people were united in worship.

When he completed the rosary, Monsignor Grace went back to Vincent, held out his hand, leaned in to him, and spoke in his ear. The only sign of surprise was a stiffening of Vincent's back and a shifting of his gaze as he searched for me. I merely nodded. I was counting on Monsignor Grace to play his part, and so far it was working.

He stooped to talk to Rachel and picked up Ellen. With no effort, he offered Rachel a hand up and tucked it into the crook of his arm. Whatever he said to the darling little girl made both her and her mother laugh as he carried Ellen out of the room, promising to get her a cold drink.

Winnie breathed a sigh of relief. "Did I tell you lately that you're a genius?"

"Only about a hundred times today."

At that moment Josiah and four other policemen entered the visitation room. They made for Vincent, but Carlo stuck his chest out and started to block their entrance. To his surprise, Vincent held him back.

"Let them come to us," he said.

"But this is disrespectful."

"*Basta!* We must show our grief and our independence but not with force. Not tonight."

Josiah gave Carlo a short nod of recognition, but put out his hand to Vincent. "You know why I'm here."

"Yes."

"There'll be no trouble?"

"Not from me."

"Thank you."

Josiah turned and jerked his head to his men. Within a heartbeat they had surrounded Mark Branch, Rachel's husband, Vincent's accountant. They jerked his hands behind his back and put handcuffs on him.

No one in the room moved. They probably weren't even breathing.

"Mark Branch, you are under arrest for the murders of Donato Ricci, Pietro DiSilva, Amadeo Santini, Paolo Santini, Catherine Ricci, Salvatore Carcieri, and Kathleen Killian."

Well, someone was finally moving. Ella screamed *"No!"* and rushed forward, clawing at the policemen. Carlo—finally able to do something—pulled her off none too gently and held her immobile until another officer slipped handcuffs on her wrists. All the while she screamed invectives until spittle ran down her chin. Winnie went to sit by Anna, holding her hand to comfort her in her confusion.

Rachel flew into the room, took one look at her husband, and whimpered. She reached out her hands and took three steps forward, but Monsignor Grace held her back. "What's happening? Why are they doing this?"

"Come with me, my dear," the monsignor said. "I'll try to explain everything. You don't want to scare your daughter."

It had all gone according to my plan, except for one thing. I craned my neck and found the face I was looking for. "Josiah. The woman in the blue coat trying to get out of the room."

He motioned to one of his men, who stopped Donato's housekeeper from leaving.

Mrs. Beltri, who had been watching the proceedings with awe, finally focused her gaze on Mark Branch. She blinked and shook her head, probably to clear her vision, to be absolutely certain of what she was seeing. The resemblance finally sank into her consciousness. *"Figlio di marcellaio? Dio mio! Figlio di marcellaio!"*

Her daughter turned to me. "She said . . ."

"I know what she said. Mark Branch is the son of Marco Ramo, the Butcher of Capodimonte."

Epilogue

Vincent invited us and everyone who had been involved in unraveling the mystery to a private reception following the funeral on Monday. His home was a huge Victorian on a tree-lined street behind Brown University on the East Side of Providence. Like many Italian families in Rhode Island, he had bought up two entire blocks that stood on dead-end streets; and the other houses were occupied by Tiny, Richard, Rachel, and the sons of his father's partners. It was an enclave that could be closed off when they wanted it to be or wide open, as it was today.

When we arrived, Dante raced to welcome us, throwing his arms around my waist and hugging me hard. "You did it! I knew you would."

"It wasn't just me. Richard and Tiny, Winnie and your Uncle Carlo, and even Monsignor Grace worked hard to find out the truth for you."

"I know. Dad told me. I wish *Nonno* hadn't died, though."

"I know. He really loved you, you know."

"Yeah, I know. Dad gave me his grey cap, but we put it away until I'm old enough to wear it."

Oh, Lord, please be with this good little boy. Make him a man like Richard. Help him to know what's right and wrong. His father is good to him, but there are things he does that scare me and make me despair for his soul. Yes, I'm sure You know about all that. Okay, I can leave it in Your hands. You don't have to shout. What do You mean, sometimes I don't hear You unless You do? Wasn't it You who told us to listen to the still small voice? Well, You do have a sense of humor. It's very, very nice to know that.

Dante tugged me by the hand past a large front parlor and into a glass-enclosed conservatory filled with green plants. There was even an orange tree! Vincent rose to take my hand, and there was some fumbling as Dante didn't want to let go. Finally, Vincent ruffled his son's hair and indicated a white rattan sofa with soft green and white cushions.

"What can I get you, Sisters?" Carlo asked. "We have orange juice with a splash of Asti, tea, coffee, wine and mixed drinks."

"I'll take the juice and Asti," I said.

"Sister Winifred?"

"I'll have the same."

"We'll have a late lunch as soon as everyone arrives," Vincent said. "Meantime, I'd like to personally thank you for what you did."

"I did it for Dante."

"We know, but it benefited us all, and that is a service our entire family will not forget."

Carlo brought us our drinks and a plate of small stuffed mushrooms and green grapes.

We chatted about the weather and the new plans Bishop Keough had for expanding Catholic schools in the state so that every community would have at least one.

Tiny drifted in and Monsignor Grace brought a surprise— Mother Frances. We smiled at each other, and I was astonished that I was actually happy to see her again. I never thought I would miss her, but I had; and I would let her know how much she had been missed, just as soon as we got back to the convent. The final guests arrived with Richard. Mrs. Beltri and her daughter gawked at their surroundings but soon relaxed and chatted easily, with a little help with Italian translation from all the Italians in the room, including Dante.

Lunch was served in a dining room that could have seated twenty comfortably, but we gathered at one end of the table so we could talk. The food was catered from Capodimonte Ristorante. We dined on a seafood chowder, fried calamari, a lovely antipasto, fusilli with three different sausages, baked cod, stuffed artichokes and a fruit and cheese platter. Coffee topped the meal.

Mrs. Beltri asked to be excused, and Winnie accompanied her to the rest room. When she had left, her daughter hinted that the old lady needed to go home. Richard went outside to find a driver for her and the two women left, with profuse thanks for a wonderful lunch and the gifts that Vincent had been heaping on them, including the daily meals.

After they left, the caterer poured and distributed fresh coffee and Dante asked to be excused. As soon as he was out of the room, Vincent said, "So how did you do it?"

"Winnie always jokes about my fixation on Plato's *Allegory of the Cave*. She's right in a way. I am fixated on it. So much so that I always look for the truth underneath the façade everyone shows to the world. I don't know why I know when someone is lying or when something is a pageant staged for good effect. I don't always see it right away, because we only ever see bits and pieces. But when the most important piece comes up—the one that's going to lead to the answer—I can see the rest begin to tumble into the blank spots, filling in the holes. There were way too many holes in this case. We were being fed a pack of lies and evasions. I started to disbelieve everything and found I could believe only some things—really, only one thing.

"I could believe Donato, and that was the key. He was dying. He knew it. I knew it. He had no reason to lie, so he didn't. Because he didn't, I had to look at everything from a different perspective. You see, Vincent, he told me about the organization. About how it started and how it works today. About how he and his three friends had done dreadful things in order to right a wrong. He didn't tell me about Ramo, not directly. But he hinted that there was something in his past that others would find despicable but that was absolutely necessary at the time. It was this information that made me wonder if everything was connected, including Kitty's death."

"There isn't any connection between her and Donato or her and Mark Branch," Monsignor Grace said. "I finally heard from Ireland. You were right about her. She did have a part in killing those two girls."

"Poor Kitty—or whatever her name was. She'd been masquerading as a maid. Masquerade. That's what began it, you know," I said. "No, Dante began it. And then we found out Catherine was murdered. I had to ask myself if hers was a random killing and couldn't believe that it was, especially not after we discovered the cyanide connection and the attempt on Vincent. It couldn't be a coincidence. It had to be deliberate. So, I looked for a motive."

"And Donato gave you one," Winnie said.

"Yes. He died tying the pieces together. Without those photos and the writing on the backs we would never have known what had happened in Italy. Without Mrs. Beltri, we would never have known about the rapes and murders of young girls and boys, one of them your aunt, Vincent. Without Mrs. Beltri's heart-wrenching testimony of how the butcher always took his cap off before he raped the girls—and made them wear it while he raped them—we would never have known the meaning that grey cap has, and why Mark had to get it back at any cost, which over the past few days included Salvatore Carcieri's and Donato's lives."

"And the lives of my father and cousins," Tiny said.

"Yes. So much for so little. A cap that denotes the Butcher

and the chief of the village. A boning knife that probably helped cut up Mrs. Beltri's cousin, and was the Butcher's favorite weapon. But it was the coat of arms that helped the most, because it contained the information about the murders in Italy and eventually led to the connection between Mark Branch and Marco Ramo, the Butcher. So much for so little."

"What about the differences in the coat of arms?" Winnie asked. "You didn't explain that."

"Oh. Well, the chicken was changed by Donato. Originally, it was the brown hen of his village, like Vincent's coat shows. But Donato said he loved the Rhode Island Red rooster's colors. Thought it suited him more."

"That would be just like him," Carlo said. "He loved dressing the dandy."

"Like father, like son," Richard said, and we all joined in his laughter.

Vincent poured himself another cup of coffee. "And the double-headed coin and fleur de lis?"

"The two-headed coin for the Butcher. The two-faced man that he was. A butcher by day, a murderer by night. I suppose Donato wanted to remember what could happen if he allowed his power to go too far. The fleur de lis, of course, was for his three partners. He honored them all his life. In his last real conversation with me, he had nothing but praise for the courage they had when they faced down the Butcher. You see, everyone else who had tried to deal with him had died. And they were only teenagers. One of them had only just been confirmed."

"My cousin Paolo."

"They were true family, he said. Protectors of the poor and the helpless."

"So Donato helped you protect the poor and the helpless one more time before he died," Monsignor Grace said. "That last conversation did much good."

"Yes. And I can't help but think there was an invisible presence guiding us—to keep this little corner of His world from becoming another hellish playground for the son of the Butcher."

"He didn't see it coming," Vincent said.

I laughed. "Neither did you!"

"And you got all that from our father?" Carlo asked.

"I got it from him and from Mrs. Beltri, whose memory is sharp about those pain-filled days. She kept referring to the Butcher as Ramos. I looked it up in the Italian dictionary that Richard gave me. It means branch. We knew the killer had access to the farm, could impersonate Vincent, had too much knowledge to be anyone outside the family, and was ruthless. Like father, like son? Why not? And there was a Branch in *this* family—Mark Branch. Was it only coincidence that his name was similar to the Butcher's? I couldn't see how so many coincidences could occur at one time. I don't believe in coincidence. I believe that there are forces at work in everything we do, that everything is connected."

"Well, that takes care of Mark. But how did you connect Ella to him?"

"First, it was the shooting. When I saw that there were shots coming from two sides of the car, I realized there was more than one of them. And since the police had been at the farm for hours, no one would have dared set up watch with them around. So, how did they know when any of us left? They had to be on the grounds. The only thing they didn't know was that we, not Vincent, were in his car. That was a big mistake on their part."

"So she started looking at who it could be who was helping Mark Branch," Winnie said.

"Yes. And that led to one of my burning questions. Mark has been married to Rachel for twelve years and he's been in this country longer than that. Why strike now? The only answer I could come up with was that he was waiting for someone to join him—his accomplice."

"Ella," Vincent said.

"Correct. Donato sent for her and Anna a few years ago, just before Donato's partners started to 'die.' As the pieces started to fall together, I had to ask myself, *if there's a father, is there also a mother?* Someone like the girls Mrs. Beltri told us about, who were raped repeatedly by the Butcher and his cohorts and then either murdered or sold into sexual slavery. Hence, all those names—both girls and boys—that were marked *disappeared* on the backs of the photos. In that kind of situation, a girl has to be very special. She has to be either very strong or sexual to survive multiple rapes. I think she—Ella—was both. The others were killed or sold out, but she stayed long enough to get pregnant. Ironically, the Butcher was defeated and killed by Donato and the others before she gave birth. She hated them as only a woman can hate; so when she had a son, she groomed him to take revenge against his father's killer. I'm not even sure she told Mark the truth about his father. It doesn't matter, of course. He made his own path, and it led to multiple murders."

I sighed at all the heartache hate could cause. "Ella's deranged, you know, the way men came home from the Great War and are now unable to function in this world. She lived in her head, thinking that murder would get them the prestige and respect and, yes, power that the Butcher had had. It was probably her idea to have Mark take an English name that mimicked his father's. Her idea to have him marry the sister of your wife. Her idea about the rat poison—which, as Carlo and Winnie know after their recent work in the laboratory yesterday morning, was the stuff I found in the boathouse. Her idea to enlist the help of the housekeeper by paying her huge sums of money, although even meager sums of money would have done the trick. But Mark had charge of your finances, Vincent. So she had access to piles of cash like those you keep in your safe at the farm. People will sell their souls for money, and the housekeeper did. But those two sold their souls for wrath and envy and pride. They used up three of the seven deadly sins. Although I believe that God is a loving father, I think there is a limit to what He will ignore. They've exceeded their limit."

I played with my napkin, trying not to cry. "It was all such a waste! I don't mean to make this sound awful, but most of the people they killed were going to die soon anyway. But those two, mother and son, their souls were so warped that they couldn't wait for nature to take its course. No, they needed to watch their victims die, some in really gruesome ways—ways that Ella must have learned when she was held captive by the Butcher. Let's hope this kind of human being is an aberration and no one else comes along who can do things like this and get away with it."

"Sister Agnes," Mother Frances said, "even if that happens, with you around people like that don't stand a chance."

AUTHOR ACKNOWLEDGMENTS

I hope you enjoyed this latest escapade of gun-toting Sister Agnes. She's part of my family, now. Many's the time that one of us in our family says *That's what Aggie would do!*

For those of you who might be taking a trip to New England—go to Federal Hill in Providence. It's changed, yes; but you can still see the old way of life, the joy of the people who live and lived there, and Venda's, the best place to get pasta, bar none. If you need any encouragement go to www. Vendaravioli.com.

Writing an historical novel about Rhode Island would be impossible without the amazing series on the history of Rhode Island that the *Providence Journal* wrote. They brought it back to life for me—and I hope for you. Many thanks to the contributing editors.

And many thanks also to my reading friends and critique group: Cameron Nyhen, Marilyn Trent, Susan Dudics-Dean, Rebecca McTavish, Judi Fadeley, Keely Thrall and Leigh Horne. Your encouragement and gentle criticism make me a better writer.

And to Bill, who reads what I write and loves every word. Every moment is precious to me.

★ ★ ★ ★ ★

RECIPES
FROM
FEDERAL
HILL

★ ★ ★ ★ ★

STEFANO'S SHORTIES SIMPLIFIED

1 pound Italian sausage, cut in small pieces
1 red pepper, sliced thin
1 green pepper, sliced thin
1 medium yellow onion, sliced thin
1 long submarine loaf of Italian bread or baguette

Fry sausage, peppers, and onions in small amount of olive oil until cooked well.
Hollow out the bread and fill with fried mixture.
Cut in 2″ pieces and serve hot as appetizers.

SISTER WINIFRED'S FAVORITE OH, SO HEAVENLY RICE PIE

1 1/2 cups milk
2 1/2 cups cooked long grain rice
10 beaten eggs
3/4 cup sugar
2 tsp. vanilla extract

Preheat oven to 325°.
Line deep dish pie pan with uncooked pie crust. Set aside.
Mix all ingredients together. Pour into prepared pie crust.
Bake for 45 minutes or until knife stuck in center comes out clean.
If desired, top with whipped topping.

TINY DISILVA'S MONUMENTALLY MEMORABLE MUSHROOM SALAD

1 pound mixed mushrooms (button, shitake, etc.)
Olive oil
Garlic wine vinegar
2 Tbs. Italian seasoning mix
Salt
1 whole garlic clove, each segment skinned
Sterilized canning jars

Cut up large mushrooms and stems. Leave small mushrooms whole.
Steam mushrooms in steamer for five minutes using small amount of salted water. Drain well.
Measure the amount of mushrooms. Divide that number in half.
Add that amount of oil to fry pan.
Add half that amount of vinegar to oil.
Heat slowly until lukewarm.
Add garlic and Italian seasoning mix.
Add mushrooms and keep very hot.
Pack mushrooms with one segment of garlic and oil mixture into sterilized jars.
Cover and cool. Keep in refrigerator.

OR: Process in water bath for 40 minutes. Store in cool place. Check often for spoilage.

OR: Freeze in small containers. Defrost in refrigerator overnight before serving.

ANNA SANTINI'S UNFORGETTABLE ITALIAN FRIED COOKIES

2 eggs
1 Tbs. sugar
1/2 tsp. salt
1/2 tsp. cardamom
1 cup milk
1 1/2 cups flour
Confectioners' sugar
Corn or peanut oil
Italian rosette iron

Beat eggs lightly.
Add next 5 ingredients and mix thoroughly. Batter will be thick like cream.

Heat oil in deep fryer or large, deep fry pan to 375°.
Heat iron in oil according to directions on rosette iron box.
Drain excess oil.
Dip iron into batter and fry in oil, shaking iron slightly until rosette falls off iron.
Repeat until surface of oil is filled with cookies.
Fry until golden brown.
Drain well.
Sprinkle with confectioners' sugar.

SAINTS PRESERVE US
SPINACH PIES

1 large can chopped spinach
Or 3 lbs fresh spinach, cooked very well
1/4 to 1/2 lb. pepperoni sausage, cut in very small pieces
 (remove skin)
1 small can sliced black olives
2 cloves fresh garlic, chopped fine
1 lb. fresh or frozen bread dough
Or 2 rolls refrigerated dough
Olive oil
Salt and pepper

Preheat oven to 400°.

Drain canned or cooked spinach very well.

Roll out bread dough. Cut into 5″ circles.

Put a good spoonful of spinach in center of bread dough circles.

Add a few pieces of pepperoni and small amount of chopped garlic to taste.

Top with a few black olives.

Sprinkle with a few drops of olive oil.

Season with salt and pepper to taste. Note: fresh spinach will need more salt than canned.

Fold filled circle in half. Place on oiled cookie sheet.

Brush tops with a little olive oil.

Bake for 20–25 minutes or until dough is crusty and golden brown.

SISTER AGNES' FAVORITE STUFFED MUSHROOMS

1 lb. large button mushrooms
1/2 cup plain bread crumbs
1 Tbs. parsley flakes
1 tsp. garlic powder
1 Tbs. dried onion flakes
1 tsp. dried basil
1/4 cup grated parmesan cheese
Salt and pepper
Water

Wipe mushrooms with slightly dampened towel IF they need it. Pull off the stem, slice the bottom off carefully, not taking too much flesh.

Put the stems in food processor.

Add the bread crumbs, and pulse until stems are coarsely ground and combination is well mixed.

Remove processor top.

Transfer mixture into bowl.

Add garlic powder, onion flakes, basil and parmesan cheese and stir to mix.

Add bread crumbs and stir well.

Add water, a little at a time until the mixture holds together.

Fill mushroom caps with mixture.

Broil for 4–7 minutes or until mixture is nicely browned on top.

Note: DO NOT WASH YOUR MUSHROOMS. THEY'RE LIKE A SPONGE AND WILL SOAK UP THE WATER, MAKING THEM HARD TO WORK WITH, AND NOT SO TASTY.

ABOUT THE AUTHOR

Barbara Cummings is an award-winning author of fifteen published novels (comedy, mystery, romance, and young adult), three short stories, and seven poems.

In 1993, her mystery novel set in Victorian London (*Dead As Dead Can Be*) was voted one of the top ten bestselling original paperbacks by Mid-Atlantic Independent Mystery Booksellers. In 1994, she received the *Romantic Times* Reviewers' Choice Award for *Prime Time*. She is also a recipient of the Washington Romance Writers' Outstanding Achievement Award. She is a member of Phi Kappa Phi Honor Society, Romance Writers of America, Mystery Writers of America, Novelists Inc, and Washington Romance Writers.

Mrs. Cummings received an MA in English from the University of Rhode Island, studied for her doctorate, and currently teaches English and Writing at Shepherd University in Shepherdstown, West Virginia. She lives nearby with her husband of forty-seven years. Mrs. Cummings can be reached at www.thecummingsstudios.com.